FAKING IT
TO MAKING IT

BY
ALLY BLAKE

MILLS &
BOON

First published in Great Britain 2013
by Mills & Boon, an imprint of Harlequin (UK) Limited.
Harlequin (UK) Limited, Eton House, 18-24 Paradise Road,
Richmond, Surrey TW9 1SR

© Ally Blake 2013

ISBN: 978 0 263 90038 5

Harlequin (UK) policy is to use papers that are natural, renewable
and recyclable products and made from wood grown in sustainable
forests. The logging and manufacturing process conform to the
legal environmental regulations of the country of origin.

Printed and bound in Spain
by Blackprint CPI, Barcelona

"Faking it in front of a guy's family is hardly a common occurrence in my life. How about yours?"

Nate's sensuous mouth grew flat, his stare much the same.

"No, didn't think so." Saskia reached for the top button of his shirt, her hand hovering an inch from his chest. "May I?"

"May you what?"

"Ruffle you up a little."

He breathed deep, his chest lifting till the weave of his luxurious woollen jacket brushed the hairs of her arms, creating skitters of…*something* all the way to her elbows.

His gaze finally left his family home to connect with hers. The tangle of blue was enough to take her breath clean away.

"Ruffle away."

0135736635

In her previous life Australian author **Ally Blake** was at times a cheerleader, a maths tutor, a dental assistant and a shop assistant. In this life Ally is a bestselling multi-award-winning novelist who has been published in over twenty languages, with more than two million books sold worldwide.

She married her gorgeous husband in Las Vegas—no Elvis in sight, although Tony Curtis did put in a special appearance—and now Ally and her family, including three rambunctious toddlers, share a property in the leafy western suburbs of Brisbane, with kookaburras, cockatoos, rainbow lorikeets and the occasional creepy-crawly. When not writing she makes coffees that never get drunk, eats too many M&Ms, attempts yoga, devours *The West Wing* reruns, reads every spare minute she can, and barracks ardently for the Collingwood Magpies footy team.

You can find out more at her website www.allyblake.com

Recent titles by the same author:

THE SECRET WEDDING DRESS
THE RULES OF ENGAGEMENT
THE WEDDING DATE

Dear Reader

When the hero in this book, Nate Mackenzie, first appeared on the page in my last book, THE SECRET WEDDING DRESS, he was such a doll. Such a charming, industrious, energetic foil for that hero—big, bad Gabe Hamilton.

The more I got to know him, the greater my crush on the guy grew. So handsome, so funny, so strong, so resolute. And did I mention handsome? So when an idea sprang to mind about Saskia Bloom, a hopeful, helpful, sweet, bossy, left-of-centre statistician researching a piece on online dating, I thought, *Who better to throw in her unsuspecting path than my darling Nate?*

I just love having a vehicle for stories like this— joyful, warm, wacky, fresh, touching, cheeky…and hot, hot, *hot*. And I can't wait to sit down and meet my next lucky couple, who are currently tootling along, thinking life's just dandy, until—*WHAM!* I do so love my job.

For more about my books swing by my website at www.allyblake.com

Till then, happy reading!

Ally

For team Arabella Rose.

Josh, Laura, Cat, David, Sam, Kristy,
Liz, Emma & Gemma.

It was an honour and a trip, with extra sauce!

CHAPTER ONE

SASKIA BLOOM FLICKED her dark fringe out of her eyes and peered through her vintage glasses at her laptop screen before madly scribbling notes on the yellow legal pad under the mouse.

"I'll eat my shoes if you're even a day under forty," she mumbled at the photo of a guy grinning inanely back at her from the Dating By Numbers website.

Undeterred, StudMuffin33 kept on smiling, as if the dauntingly athletic profile was so appealing any woman would let the age-fib slip.

Favourite Movie: The Fast and the Furious
Collects: surfboards
Who'd Play You in the Movie of Your Life? Jason Statham
Looking for: an open-minded lady with a twinkle in her eye

Good lord.
Mouse hover and click.
The photo of the next guy gave her such a fright she flinched. BirdLover28 had tufty hair, wore a grimace rather than a smile and had a chicken on his shoulder. A live one, she hoped.

Favourite TV Show: Dr Who (the original!)
Sundays are for: garage sales

Celebrity Crush: Tyra Banks
Looking for: fun in all the wrong places

Alas, Saskia would not be partaking of said fun. For, even though it had been several months since she'd been booted back into the dating pool, she wasn't online looking for The One. Or a "Saturday night special" as one possibility had so gallantly offered.

Her account with Dating By Numbers was research, pure and simple. She and her business partner, Lissy—together known as SassyStats—had been hired by the site to collate a fun statistical analysis of online dating. In order to do the best job possible, she'd jumped from an aeroplane for a piece on adrenalin junkies. Dived with sharks for a study on phobias. In comparison, creating a dating profile was cushy.

Saskia lifted her booted foot to the chair, wrapped an arm around her woolly-tights-clad knee, and, chewing on the end of a pen, shook her head at the dozen more possibilities in her inbox.

Research or not, it *was* actually pretty flattering.

With her wavy brown hair, her mother's olive skin, eyes that were kind of brown and a lean frame that puberty had pretty much ignored, under the right lighting, with humidity low, she could *just* about pull off cute. The idea that so many guys had considered her for a follow up email was a marvel.

If she'd known *this* was the response she'd get, she'd have signed up long ago! She'd met *Stu* in a *pub,* and look how *that* had turned out.

There he'd sat hunched in his old coat, looking so dark and mysterious, with pen smudges on his fingertips. He'd looked as if he'd needed a warm meal and a hug. Turned out he'd needed her mobile phone, her TV, her computers, her appliances and more. In recompense he'd left a nasty note, a huge debt and his dog.

Saskia glanced over at Ernest, the big wiry Airedale currently lying on his back, legs in the air, snoring on the dinky old armchair in the corner of her office.

With a sigh, she slid her feet back to the floor and shifted the legal pad an inch. She and Ernest might have discovered a bona fide fondness for one another, but she'd never get used to the angry red envelopes that fell through her mail-slot on a weekly basis. Never wanted to. The only way to make them go away was to work. And work some more. And then, when night fell and her bed was beckoning, get back to work.

Mouse hover and click.

Saskia lifted her hand off the mouse, ready to take notes on the next candidate, but at the sight of him her hand wobbled pointlessly in midair.

She might, in fact, have gasped at the sight, because Ernest suddenly snorted, his legs twitching like an up-ended spider, before settling back into a dream-filled sleep.

Gorgeous didn't even begin to describe the man. Drop-dead, movie star, take-your-breath-away gorgeous came a *tiny* bit closer. The shot was candid, with the man looking at something over the photographer's shoulder. Dark blond hair precision cut. Sleeves of a pale blue business shirt neatly rolled up to his upper arms, a vein or two roping from wrist to elbow. A solitary raised eyebrow, a barely there lift to one corner of a truly sensuous mouth. But who'd even notice, considering the guy had the bluest eyes Saskia ever seen.

How does a man who looks like that not have someone in his life? she wondered. Though, considering the fibs the other men had told, she couldn't count on it!

He did look resolute, as if he wouldn't be used to hearing the word no, so maybe he was plain mean. Or into cross-stitching. Or he had halitosis. Or really gnarly toenails. Or maybe he was looking for something even more outrageous than "fun in all the wrong places."

Intrigue levels rising, Saskia wriggled the blood back into

her fingers and scrolled to the mini-profile that had been sent out with the guy's initial contact.

Favourite Book: Catch-22
Drink of choice: double espresso
Thing you say more than any other: Next
Looking for: a wedding date, no strings

Pretty much bang-on to his picture, which was an anomaly unto itself. And Saskia did love an anomaly. That love had sent her from pure statistics into research in the first place. That moment reminded her why, as a seed of an idea sprang to life inside her.

Lifting her backside from her chair, she flicked through a pile of random papers till she found the press release Marlee at Dating By Numbers had sent over as part of the initial brief.

The number of people who had signed on—and only to that one site—was staggering. All of them had struggled using traditional avenues in their search for companionship, for sex, for love. Including her. And if a man who loved coffee as much as she did, had awesome taste in literature, and looked enough like a young Paul Newman to induce a drool epidemic had reached his thirties without finding someone, what *would* it take?

She'd been looking for an angle for her infographic, and she might just have found one.

When a massive Big Bang Theory mug appeared next to Saskia's elbow, she nearly jumped out of her skin. "God, you scared me half to death!"

"Not surprised. You have that weird scientist look in your eyes," said Lissy. The blue and purple tips of her long blonde locks bounced as she landed with a *whump* in the bouncy chair on her side of the paint-splattered old table they used as an office desk. "If it was legal I'd marry your espresso machine."

"Get in line." Saskia put her glasses on the desk, blinked to clear her eyes and, breathing in the rich scent of the cocoa enriched brew, let the huge mug warm her hands before closing her eyes and taking a sip. After Stu had taken off with everything she'd leased computers but bought a replacement espresso machine. Horse before the cart and all that.

"So, what are we working on?" asked Lissy. "The railway map thing? The business listing thing?"

"The online dating thing."

"Ooh, much more fun."

"I'll drink to that." They clinked mugs. "I think I've just had a bit of a breakthrough. I'm considering adding something extra to my analysis—along the lines of an equation for finding love."

Lissy stopped sipping at her coffee and blinked. "Like, chocolates plus flowers multiplied by heaps of hot sex equals never having to say you're sorry?"

Saskia laughed as she scrawled curlicues in the top corner of her legal pad, her mind whizzing now it had hit on something. "Not quite. Mathematics is natural. Love is natural. It only makes sense that it's *mathematically* quantifiable."

Lissy glanced pointedly at the pile of bills on Saskia's side of the desk which, for the first time *ever* included a late mortgage payment.

"I wouldn't be making work for myself, as I'm doing the research anyway," Saskia said. "And I think it would make a great anchor for the bottom of the infographic."

Then again, maybe Lissy was right. If Saskia wanted to wrestle back control of her mortgage payments, let alone get back to the renovations she'd been in the middle of doing when Stu absconded, she needed to focus.

Unfortunately, while Lissy was a crazy brilliant graphic artist, to her, *focus* was a foreign word. "It's never been done? This love formula thing?"

"Maybe," Saskia said, enthusiasm spiking again. "Or maybe nobody's ever tried. Perhaps somebody just needed inspiration."

"Like when Einstein was hit with that apple."

"Newton."

"Whatever. So, what hit *you?*"

"Nothing hit me." Saskia made the mistake of glancing at her laptop.

Lissy's eyes narrowed. Then, quick as a rattlesnake, she spun her chair round the desk and looked over Saskia's shoulder before she had the chance to snap the thing closed.

"Ha!" Lissy pointed. "Talk about inspiration. Who is *that?*"

Saskia's eyes skewed back to the monitor, to the bluest eyes and the hint of what would have amounted to an indecently sensuous smile if the photographer had only been kind enough to wait half a second more. "His handle is NJM."

"Handle? He's one of our online dating guys?" Lissy blew out a long, slow whistle. "Why did I let you be the guinea pig on this one?"

"Because you were dating Dropkick Dave and when he saw you smile at the greengrocer he snapped all your carrots in half."

Lissy winced at the memory. "I'll admit the guy was high strung—"

Saskia coughed out a laugh at the understatement of the year.

"—but Lordy the man knew how to kiss." With that Lissy disappeared into a daze. Saskia made a mental note to check Lissy's phone and make sure Dropkick Dave had been deleted.

With a shake of her head Lissy came to, tiptoed her chair back to her side of the table, and angling her mug at the back of Saskia's laptop, said, "Stats please."

Saskia shuffled the mouse and clicked on the link for NJM's full online profile. The sight of neat and tidy columns, of horizontal bars filled with information, of questions with answers, and she found her zen. "Six-two. Blue eyes. Dark blond hair. Financier. No interests listed."

Well, now, *that* just seemed a little sad.

"I put up my hand to give him some!" said Lissy.

Saskia laughed, then realised she was still rolling a finger over the mouse like a caress.

She lifted her hand and cricked her fingers. She was mid-knuckle-crack on her second hand when Lissy came out with, "Screw research. You should date him. For real."

Saskia's mouth twisted sideways. She noticed that her hand was on the mouse again, and it had somehow shifted till the little arrow hovered over the bright yellow button with the happy-fonted "Why not?" scripted inside of it.

Why not? "He's not my type."

"Honey, he's everybody's type. And don't even try to tell me you wouldn't be his. You've got that sexy geek girl thing that's so hot right now. And if he's on that site, he's looking for love."

"First, this is a job, not a cattle call. Second, he's not looking for love—he's looking for a wedding date. Third, for all we know this is one of twenty dating sites he's listed on and he's completely indiscriminate."

"Wow. Strident, much?"

Saskia breathed out long and hard. "Lissy—"

"I know, I know. You'll get there when you're ready. But, sweetheart, how long has it been since What's-his-name decamped?"

Saskia glanced at Ernest and in a stage whisper said, "Seven months."

Lissy whispered back. "The dog can't understand English."

"Oreos," Saskia said, this time at a normal decibel level.

Ernest woke with such a start he fell off the armchair. Three seconds later he was at Saskia's side, paws on her lap, claws stretching out the zigzags on her woollen tights in the hope of finding cookie crumbs.

"Later, baby," she said, ruffling his ears, and sending him back to the chair with a pat on the bum.

"Way I see it, this is your chance to try something new." Lissy reached out and turned Saskia's monitor so she could get a better look at the man thereupon. "Not some indigent fixer-upper, but a guy who's sexy and brilliant. A man who looks like he knows how to take care of himself for once. And take care of you, if you know what I mean?"

Lissy finished with a Groucho-style eyebrow-wiggle, then slurped at her coffee, shuffled in her chair and got to work.

Saskia tried to do the same, cracking the spine of a fresh yellow legal pad, writing "Dating By Numbers" at the top and "Love Formula" beneath. She crossed it out, tried to think of a more appropriate title and, no thanks to Lissy, couldn't.

Also thanks to Lissy, her mind kept curling back to the same conversation she and Lissy had had a million times over. Lissy postulating that Saskia's yen for needy guys came down to a childhood spent trying, without much success, to lighten the life of her clueless, maths professor, single dad. Saskia contending that she simply liked who she liked. And if that happened to be men who made her feel indispensable, then what was wrong with that?

Apart from the fact that it never lasted.

Her gaze swept back to the screen and she let it trail over every inch of *yum.*

NJM looked like the least needy man on the planet. But could he kiss a girl so well she'd forgive him for snapping her carrots? *Yeah,* she thought, tingles curling into existence inside her belly, *I have a feeling he could.*

But that wasn't why she clicked on the happy yellow "Why not?" button on NJM's email. She had a job to do—a well-paying job. NJM was an anomaly in the heretofore predictability of the remainder of subjects in her study and therefore worth investigating further.

And while she had more work than she would ever have taken on at one time under normal circumstances, a girl had to eat.

Weddings did it every time.

It had taken years, diligence and dogged immovability, but

Nate Mackenzie had finally trained his sisters to leave him well enough alone when it came to his confirmed bachelorhood. Until a wedding invite arrived in the mail. Then all bets were off.

He'd just hung up from his oldest sister, Jasmine, when the twins, Faith and Hope, came at him, conference-call-style.

"She's *lovely!*" one of them exclaimed before even emitting a hello.

He leant back in his office chair, executed a half turn till the sunshine slashing past the Melbourne skyline and through the intimidating wall of windows nearly blinded him. "I'm fine, thanks. You?"

Ignoring his sarcasm, the twins tag-teamed. "Jasmine's friend makes the best macaroons."

"I've seen photos. She's just your type."

He opened his mouth to ask just what his type might be, but he snapped his mouth shut at the last second.

They were good at finding weak spots. He was better.

After all, he'd taught them all they knew: a consequence of becoming the man of the house at fifteen.

He pressed his feet to the floor and a thumb to the temple that had begun to throb. "I'm thrilled you are all so content in your own lives that you have the time to stick your collective noses into mine, but you need to focus your impressive energies elsewhere. Third World hunger, perhaps?"

"But—"

"No more set-ups. Consider that an order."

At that, a pause. Then lashings of laughter which had his other temple throbbing in syncopated rhythm against the first.

When they shifted into a familiar tune about how his natural born charm and adorable baby blues wouldn't get him by for ever, Nate slowly turned his chair back to face his vast office as his brain flicked through possible ways to convince them to leave the subject of finding him a good woman the hell alone. He could honestly beg work, but that was nothing new. A weekend was something other people had. He hadn't set foot on a beach in so long he couldn't remember how sand felt between his toes. And telling them he was only keen on bad women hadn't stopped them before; it had merely expanded the pond from which they fished on his behalf.

"I'm seeing someone!" The walls of Nate's vast office seemed to heave away from him as the import of the words he'd just uttered echoed into the ensuing silence. Damn twins—they were like a pair of hammers banging at an exposed nerve. It had been bound to jerk eventually.

But when the silence deepened, Nate wondered if he'd hit on something inspired. If he oughtn't to have invented a significant other years ago—someone who travelled often, was ethically against telephones, who had lost her whole family in some tragic accident so he could therefore never subject his love to the pain of meeting his.

Caught up in his own daydreams of freedom, he realised his chance to hang up on a high a moment too late.

One twin said, "Someone who can string a sentence together without saying 'um'?"

"What the hell do I care?" he heard himself bellow. "So long as she looks good, smells nice and goes home happy."

"Nate," they said on twin sighs, with familiar waves of guilt pouring down the phone line. They *knew* they should be nicer, considering all he'd sacrificed to make sure they were well-adjusted after their father died. Knowing didn't make it so. They had stubborn Mackenzie genes after all.

"The worst part is I don't think you're kidding," said one.

"That the perfect Nate date wants no commitment, no happy-ever-after, no way," said the other.

"Find *her* for me and then we can talk," said Nate as his office door swung open. Gabe poked his head through the gap. Done with being outnumbered, Nate waved his recently returned business partner in with a brisk flap of his hand.

One raised eyebrow later, Gabe shut the door behind him

and ambled across the room to lower his huge form into a chair that would have been plenty big enough for any other man. Gabe, on the other hand, looked as if he'd need a crowbar to get out.

"I have to go," said Nate. "My ten o'clock is here."

"Say 'hi' to Gabe from me."

Then, "Tell him if it doesn't work out with Paige, he can always—"

Nate hung up before any more of *that* image made its way into his subconscious.

"The girls on the warpath?" said Gabe, as Nate once again rubbed his thumbs across both temples.

"This time, it's your fault."

"How's that, exactly?"

"If you weren't with Paige, you'd never have met Mae and Clint, who'd never have invited me to their wedding. And Macbeth's witches wouldn't have made it their life's mission to find me a woman."

Gabe's dark stare flattened. "Are you wishing away *my* woman?"

"Not," said Nate, settling back in his chair. "For years you walked around like a bear with a sore tooth. Now you're practically cuddly."

Gabe's lip curled as he as good as snarled. But then the big guy seemed to soften, sweeten, and the smile that slipped through confirmed cuddly was fine, if it meant he had *her*.

Hell.

Thankfully Nate was spared, as Gabe's mobile rang and he answered with a gruff, "Hamilton."

To think, Nate mused, it felt like only yesterday that together he and the big guy had sketched out their radical dream of a maverick venture capital business on the back of a beer coaster in a pub near uni. And now that crazy dream was a shining beacon of trust, fiscal responsibility and innovation within the morass of world-wide financial tremblings.

Nate had reached the heights he'd envisioned that long ago night, and had soared higher still. He had property all over the world, a stake in some of the most successful businesses in the country, and more money than he could count. And yet the heart of that dream, the pinnacle he'd aspired to, the moment when the pendulum of success had hit its peak and he could ease back, content with his success and enjoy the spoils, had never eventuated.

Every decision, every purchase, every paperclip was still under his tight control—as though if in letting go he'd lose it all. And it wasn't lost to him that he was nearing the age when his own hard-working father had gone to work one day and never come home.

Gabe hung up and said, "You free for lunch? The gaming guy I was telling you about is meeting me at Zuma at one, and I'm sure having us both there'll put the requisite sparkle in his eyes to get his scrawl on the dotted line."

Nate ran his hands over his face, pushing the mounting signs of frustration down deep. "I can swing by at quarter past."

"Better. Keep 'em keen." Gabe pressed himself from the chair and only when he reached the door did he look back.

"So, have you got a date for Mae and Clint's wedding, or what?" Gabe asked.

Nate lugged his stapler all the way across the room. It bounced off the wall a foot from Gabe's shoulder.

"I take it that's a no?"

Then Gabe was out through the door, leaving Nate to deal with the onset of a new range of throbs in his temples.

It *was* a no. And yet he'd told Faith and Hope he was seeing someone. When the actual truth was somewhere in between.

He'd get a damn date, if only to get them off his back for the next few weeks till the big day. But it wouldn't be anyone they knew. Or even anyone *he* knew for that matter.

Asking a woman on a date was one thing. Asking a woman to a wedding was akin to smothering himself in catnip and taking a swan dive into a pride of lionesses. There wasn't a kind way to tell someone with confetti stuck to her eyelashes that it was never going to happen.

But it *was* never going to happen.

For the six years between the day of his father's heart attack and the day his trust fund had been opened to him he'd devoted himself to being the man in his young sisters' lives. They'd repaid the favour by using his toothbrush, and wearing his shirts to bed. He'd asked them to stop and they'd acted out by dating his friends. And no matter how he'd managed to swallow it down, to let them do what they had to do, they'd cried themselves to sleep. He'd heard them, night after night, the sound tearing away at his insides. Until he'd become impervious to tears, to mood swings, to raging hormones and wily feminine ways. It was the only way he'd lived to fight another day.

Two hours after Mae had told him to "save the date," he'd tagged a research team to find him a dating website. All he'd told them was that it had to boast discretion and success; they didn't need to know why.

Since then he'd met six perfectly nice, attractive, elegant, smart women, every single one of whom had taken one look at him and sized him up for a tux, a four-bed house and a Range Rover with a reversing camera.

But time had run out.

He checked his email to find another of his "Maybes" had come back with a "Why not?"

More determined than ever, he opened the email. Her tag was Bloomin.

Favourite Pizza Topping: ham & red peppers
Favourite Music: retro grunge
If I Could Be Anywhere in the World I'd Be: right where
I am
Looking for: someone to talk to

Retro grunge? What the hell was retro grunge? Sounded dire. And yet he opened her picture for a second look. And then he remembered.

After an hour of trawling the site that first night he'd hit a point where the string of women in bikinis grinning suggestively at the camera had become a blur. He'd rather have tugged out his own eyelashes than read another thing but the very next picture that had appeared on the screen had been so unexpected it had stopped him short.

A woman in her late twenties sitting in a café, with a shaggy scarf-thing around her neck, dark hair in a messy twist that just reached one shoulder, and an old felt fedora perched on top of her head.

Nate leaned his elbow on the desk and rested his chin between thumb and forefinger. With the other hand he zoomed in till her eyes filled the screen. She was attractive, in an off-beat kind of way, with her fine chin, fine nose and soft pink lips curved into an easy smile. But those eyes of hers were something else. Wide-set, the colour hovering on the edge of brown, the long dark lashes creating sultry shadows below.

But within them was the most captivating thing about her, that one thing that had eluded him for so long… Contentment.

He wasn't sure he even knew what that felt like any more. And here, at his fingertips, was a woman who claimed to be happy being right where she was.

Without another thought he hit "Reply," picked a time, asked her to pick the place. Even if he'd built a client base on becoming on a first-name basis with some of the best chefs in town, in this case it was far better to go somewhere atypical or it would get back to his sisters.

It always did.

And a man had to have his priorities straight.

CHAPTER TWO

FOR ALL ITS family name, Mamma Rita's Italian restaurant in Fitzroy was dark, sensual and bohemian, a hotspot for artists and hipsters. If conversation was your bag the beer garden at the back rarely saw beer and reeked of the sweet smoke of the philosophical thinker. Saskia, though, loved it for the great food, and for a girl on a budget one decadent meal filled you up enough not to have to eat for another twenty-four hours.

Dolled up in her favourite batik pants, sandals made in Nepal and an upcycled scarf she'd made herself from an old T-shirt, Saskia sat fiddling with the piece of string she'd tied around her wrist to remind her of…*something* as, with scientific appreciation, she watched the man who'd just walked through the front door.

The photo of NJM hadn't lied, though it could be accused of under-representation. He looked immaculate; his dark suit crisp, the knot of his deep red tie tight, his shoulders broad and proud. And as a waitress approached the naturally provocative curve of his mouth hooked slowly into a nearly-smile. Even from across the restaurant Saskia saw the poor girl's knees buckle.

He really was beautiful. But, even better to Saskia's mind, beautifully anomalous.

It didn't make sense, and to a mathematician there was no more satisfying moment than when the seemingly senseless finally added up. Lissy dated bad boys because she wanted to drive her rich parents crazy. Ernest liked Oreos because she'd shared hers with him the day Stu had left. But why would a man who looked like that need to go online to find a date to a wedding?

Saskia ran a hand over her hair which was—by feel at least—not doing anything overly crazy. He must have caught the movement as the next moment his eyes found hers.

Wow, she thought, her lungs tightening and her tummy tripping over itself in rhapsodic pleasure, *those eyes should be classed a lethal weapon.*

He lifted his hand in a wave. She did the same.

Thus unfrozen, Saskia shuffled her fork as if it was important she do so at that very moment, and told herself to get a grip. This was research, not a real date. And if a chat with NJM of the blue eyes, dark suit and sinfully sensuous mouth could help her nail the angle that would take her infographic from informative to viral, then she'd just have to suffer through a date with the guy.

As her research subject began to stride her way Saskia made to stand. In pressing her hand to the table, her palm landed on her fork, sending it flying across the room.

Saskia watched, mouth agape, as it spun towards the table of a young couple, where it landed with a series of less-than-musical crashes, causing the girl to scream at the top of her lungs.

A pair of waiters in black and white zipped out to clear the mess, calm the girl, and offer free desserts.

"Need this?"

Saskia dragged her eyes from the disaster zone in the direction of a rumbling deep voice. Her eyes hit jacket button, rich red tie, jaw carved by the gods, a mouth tilted at the corners, a nose like something freed from Italian marble and smiling blue eyes that made the straight lines and curlicues flittering through her head scatter like bowling pins.

And then her focus shifted and she noticed he was holding a clean fork.

"Right," she said, shaking her head and laughing. "Thank you. Not one of my more elegant moments."

NJM's mouth curved into a deeper smile. It was a mouth made for smiling, she decided, amongst other things.

"Shall we?" he said, motioning to the table.

He waited for her to plonk into her chair before he eased his large frame into the seat opposite, popping his jacket button and running a hand down his perfect tie. His nails were as neat and tidy as the rest of him. His fingers were long and graceful, yet exquisitely masculine.

She lifted back out of her chair and held out a hand, "I'm Saskia. Saskia Bloom."

"Nate Mackenzie," he said, his nearly smile stretching out into the real thing, taking him from beautiful all the way to heartbreaking.

Maybe he had a third nipple. Or ate with his feet. But so far, Saskia saw no obvious reason a man like him couldn't find love on any street corner in the free world.

"A friend and I had a bit of fun guessing what the NJM stood for," Saskia said.

"Care to fill me in on your guesses for the *J*?"

Juicy, she thought. *Jpeg. Junk.* "Not so much."

The smile was back, and so were the curly tingles in her belly. *Charisma,* she told herself. Something chemical—hormonal, perhaps, or to do with endorphins. Not her field.

"Jackson," he proffered. "It was my father's name."

Her researcher's ear pricked. "Was?"

A beat, then, "He passed away several years back."

"Oh, I'm so sorry to hear that. Mine too. I mean, his name wasn't Jackson, but my father passed away a few years ago." When, Nate gave her nothing, just that face, and the promise of that smile, she blundered on. "I don't have a middle name, though. My mum died having me and it was all my father could do to name me at all. Even then it was after the doctor who'd given him the bad news. Or so went the story he told me every day on my birthday—"

Apparently she was going to blunder on till the end of time, as her research subject sure wasn't about to stop her. To stop herself, she reached for the massive jug of iced water, but Nate got there first. Perhaps it was gentlemanly behaviour. More likely, considering the fork incident, the guy was a quick learner. She sat on her hands as he poured her drink.

"So," she said, after managing a drink without spilling any on herself, "is this how your blind date's normally go? A slapstick show followed by the comparison of dead parents?"

"Not so much," he said, his smile only going as far as his eyes, which somehow didn't diminish the effect one jot. "Yours?"

"You're my first."

"Ah, a virgin."

"*Noooo*. Not for a *looong* time." Then, as it sank in, "An online dating first-timer? Yep."

She wasn't a natural blusher. Not by a long shot. But something about this guy had her blood in a spin.

"Ready to order, *cara?*" asked the owner, affectionately known as *Mr* Rita—a tall, skinny man in his sixties who sported a nifty little moustache.

Saskia shook herself upright. "Um, sorry! Haven't even looked at the menu. Can you give us another five?"

She shoved a big plastic menu at Nate to distract him from Mr Rita's not so subtle winking and thumbs up, then she set to studying the menu as if she *didn't* know the thing off by heart.

As they put their orders in with Mr Rita a few minutes later Saskia's phone rang. She didn't need to glance at it to know it was Lissy, calling in case she needed a fake emergency. She quickly switched it to "Do not answer."

"Your back-up plan?" Nate asked, motioning to a passing waiter for the wine list. "That was early."

"My what?" she said, sliding her phone into the big bag at her feet.

His eyes slid back to her. Knowing. And blue. So very, very blue.

With a laugh, she admitted, "Spot-on, smart boy. Like you didn't have me pick the restaurant so nobody you know would see us together."

For the first time his eyes lost that permanent glint and he looked honestly surprised. And for the first time she felt as if she wasn't on the back foot but leading from the front, where she much preferred to be.

"Am I wrong?" She leaned a little his way, her palms flat on the table.

"No," he said, blinking. "And now I hear out loud how that sounds I feel like I ought to apologise."

She shrugged, pointed out a bottle of red from the list in his hand. "If you'd taken one look at me and walked back out the door *then* you would have owed me an apology. It was only sensible of us both to take measures. I mean, you should see the lies the other guys on the site tell about themselves."

"Lies?" he repeated, as if it had never occurred to him.

Saskia counted off her fingers. "Your photo might have been a fake. You might have been lying about your age, your weight, your occupation, your name, your reason for joining the site. You might have been a psycho killer."

With each less-than-flattering "might have been" Nate's surprise, if anything, seemed to wane. The glint was back, and he too leaned forward. She caught a hint of purely masculine spice curling above the saucy scents of herbs and garlic.

"So, if you met a man in a bar, on a train, or jogging in the park, you'd have more faith that he wasn't a psycho killer?"

"I don't jog."

His mouth kicked, as if his smile surprised even him.

Her cheek twitched in response. He noticed, and the glint in his eyes changed. Deepened. Found some kind of heat. At which point his gaze dropped to her mouth, the dip at the bottom of her neck, then moved back to her eyes.

While Saskia struggled to remember how to breathe.

But while Nate Jackson Mackenzie, with his good looks, air of money and charm that could lure a siren to dry land, was probably used to having women fall all over themselves whenever he walked into a room, Saskia wasn't most women.

Which was why, when he stretched out a leg beneath their small table, his calf connecting with hers and shooting sparks up her leg, she said, "I didn't sign up to Dating By Numbers in an effort to find my one true love."

The slight rise of an eyebrow gave her the impression he didn't believe her.

Wow. Okay. So that irked. Maybe that was his great flaw: he could be irksome.

She whipped her bag onto her lap, found a business card and thrust it in his direction. "I'm a freelance statistical researcher working on an infographic about online dating for the website."

She could have pumped a fist in the air at the surprise that coloured his eyes at that one! And then from one heartbeat to the next his brow furrowed and she saw the brain behind those dauntingly beautiful eyes whir into life. It hadn't occurred to her that he might leave, but the longer he sat there, staring at her card, the more she wondered. And hoped that he'd stay.

He finally, *finally,* pocketed her card and said, "And to think you all but accused *me* of being a possible psycho killer."

"I'm a mathematician," she said. "Not exactly the same."

"I thought the point was that people lie."

"I— *What?*" Irked didn't even touch on how *that* made her feel. Punctuating her words with a waggly finger, Saskia said, "I said I was looking for somebody to talk to, which is completely true."

One eyebrow cocked. "Safer to say it was bending the truth?"

"Not even slightly. It's not my fault if you misunderstood my meaning."

She crossed her arms, knowing she sounded defensive. But it was hard to be all sweetness and light when he was watching her the way he was. All charm and half smiles were gone as he looked her over, as if he was sizing her up for something. Hopefully not a hole in the ground.

Then he did some surprising of his own when next he said, "My motives for dating online aren't altogether pure either."

Ignoring the "altogether pure" jab, Saskia attempted to raise an eyebrow right back at him. But she'd never mastered the skill, so probably ended up looking astounded. She schooled her features back to normal. "You said you were after a date for a wedding?"

"I am. But recent events have meant my needs have altered a little."

"Do I need to call my back-up plan?"

He laughed—a deep, rumbling sound that made her knees clench together.

"The greater problem, for me, is that I have three sisters who seem to think it's their mission in life to find me a wife. Thus, I let slip that I already have a date for the wedding, and that this date and I are…seeing one another."

"Let me get this straight. There are no women in your life who would happily go with you to a wedding, so you made one up?"

"Not one who would understand that it wasn't the beginning of something more."

Okay. Now she'd met the guy, she could see that. Saskia felt herself nodding.

He went on, "What I need, Saskia, as well as a wedding date, is someone who would be willing to pretend to be my girlfriend."

Still nodding, she realised he'd stopped talking and was looking at her intently. As if waiting for an answer.

"I'm sorry, did you say something?"

"Are you dating anyone at the moment, Saskia?"

"Am I—?" Saskia thought of Lissy, Dropkick Dave and snapped carrots. "I wouldn't have signed up to a dating site if I was."

"But you've signed up even though you're not looking for 'The One'?"

Her mouth twisted. He had her there.

"So, how do you feel about bending the truth just a little while longer?"

Saskia blinked, the meaning of his words coming through slow and sluggish. "You want to do all that…with *me?*"

His nostrils flared slightly, as if he was weighing his options one last time. Well, to hell with that. She was nobody's—

"Yes," he said with a determined nod.

"Right."

Saskia so wished she had pen and paper at hand as what-ifs, problems and possibilities, questions and escape routes burst inside her head, spearing away into a million tangents.

"But…can't you just tell your sisters no? Tell them…whatever your problem really is?"

Secret wife? Secret difficulty in the bedroom? Secret identity? She itched to ask.

But when a muscle flickered in Nate's cheek and a moment later he lifted a thumb to his right temple, she thought *best not.* Best not tell him his idea was crazy either. Pretend girlfriend. *Sheesh!* Only he didn't look crazy. He looked as if he was at the end of his rope.

And just like that the curly tingles in her belly pinged into perfect straight lines.

Could it be possible that Nate Mackenzie needed her after all?

It had been months since she'd felt that flicker of purpose. Just because one man had thrown her benefaction back in her face so cruelly, it didn't mean she wasn't damn good at it.

"You're serious?" she asked.

Nate's thumb stopped rubbing his temple and he looked her dead in the eye. Saskia tried her very best to not wriggle as all that gorgeous intensity trickled through her like over-carbonated bubbly.

"As serious as a man can be," he said.

Mr Rita and his boys arrived at that moment, with plates of colourful bruschetta and fat, shiny strips of barbecued *calamari* and green salad. But, while Saskia usually had to stop herself from leaning over and kissing the plate, her eyes never once left Nate's.

"Buon appetito!" said Mr Rita.

As one Nate and Saskia said, *"Grazie."*

And then they both smiled.

Saskia took a breath. "I'm..." *Flabbergasted, bemused, actually considering this?* "I don't know how to put this, but I'm not sure if I can pull it off. You're—not the kind of man I usually date."

"You might be surprised to know you're not the kind of woman I usually date either," said Nate, laughing as if the world had finally found its natural order.

She kind of wanted to kick him in the shin. In fact...

"Oof!" he said, sitting up and rubbing at the spot.

"Sorry." She shuffled on her seat, as if that had been her intention the whole time. "So how would this work, exactly?"

"It's the first Saturday in spring. You free?"

She did the math in her head. "I believe so."

"That's how it's done." And then he smiled, as if the deal was done. Poor love. He had no idea what he was in for.

Saskia bit into her *calamari,* enjoyed every succulent drop, before asking, "So, what do I get out of it?"

"Hmm?"

"The deal. You're getting a girlfriend..." She paused when the guy actually winced at the word.

"What do you want, Saskia?" he asked, charm forming between the words like mercury.

"I want what I wanted from the beginning. To get the low-down on online dating." But if she could save time, money, by having a guinea pig do it for her...

"Here's the low down," said Nate. "It's as much of a crap shoot as closing your eyes and picking someone out of the phone book. I should know. You're my seventh."

Her mouth dropped open. "You've asked *six* other women to pretend to date you?"

His mouth kicked into a smile while his eyes came over all dark and intense, lit with that flicker of heat. "I've been on six dates," he corrected. "I asked only you."

"Oh." Well, that was kind of nice. "But I still need first-hand experience for my study—"

He shook his head, his eyes not leaving her. "No dating between now and then. I won't either. Goes without saying."

"Good to know. But I was actually going to suggest that maybe *you* could be the subject of my piece."

A muscle flickered in his cheek and she wondered how long it would be before he was rubbing at that temple of his again. "Saskia, I'm not talking to you about my dating habits. My private life is just that. Private."

He looked as if he meant it. But Saskia had always found that men liked talking about themselves. So she wasn't really worried on that score. She'd find a way to get to the heart of the man—especially if she had a few weeks to do it. At the thought of a few weeks in the company of this man the curls of sensation were back in her belly.

"So when's our next date?" she asked.

A frown creased his brow. "The wedding."

"But what if someone asks how we met? If they ask you about my home, my family, my friends, my work? What's an infographic?"

"I'm sorry—a what?"

"An infographic. It's what I am working on for the dating site."

He looked pained.

"It's a diagram that shows information—stats, links, comparisons—in a bright, attractive, easy-to-digest contained image. We need a little background to do this properly, Nate. I can put it together, if you'd like. Research is my thing."

A list of dry questions, she thought, warming to the idea, *with some curve balls thrown in.* Classic stat-collection technique. He could tell her a lot that way without even meaning to.

"Or how long will it take for your family to think you've just made me up?" When his cheek twitched again she knew she had him. "We'll need to set up a couple of meetings between now and then. Casual get-togethers. Coffee, perhaps. We both like coffee. The Art Gallery has an Impressionists exhibition. Or we could go ice-skating. I don't mind."

Keeping him thinking about places he clearly did not want to go with her gave her the chance for the other half of her brain to create the research project in earnest. Questions piled up inside her head with such speed it made her breathless.

And as she was getting excited by the research, the layers upon layers of information this man could provide for her love formula, she remembered the pile of red envelopes wavering on her desk.

Her excitement deflated like a pricked balloon. "I don't think I can do this."

"Why not?"

The *why* was like a pain in her belly—one that was lessening by the day, but would remain till the day the last red envelope landed in her mailbox. "Time, I guess. More than anything."

"An hour together here and there should suffice," he said.

"Well, now, that's about the most romantic thing a nearly pretend boyfriend has ever said to me."

His mouth did the surprise smile thing—the one that gave a hint of straight white teeth and lit his intense eyes with genuine laughter. "What's the problem? I'm a problem-solver. It's what I do. Money, time, space, audience, you need it I provide it."

"You'd be cutting into my worktime. I need to work."

"Why?"

He was so sincere, so keen, she made a quick decision to tell him the truth. Part of it anyway. Not bend the truth, just not tell all.

"I have...debts." Yet her chin lifted as she said it.

His long, slow breath in made her stomach hurt. Then, with a nod, he said, "I'll take care of them."

She shot out a laugh so loud the table shook. "Just like that? A blank cheque?" When he didn't laugh back she realised. "You're serious?"

"Deadly."

"But I haven't even said what I owe!"

He gave a slight lift of the shoulder, as if she could name her price. "Consider this negotiation, Miss Bloom."

Miss Bloom now, was it?

"You have a debt. I have the means to wipe it from existence. I have need of a date to my friends' wedding, and you seem amenable to the terms and conditions that come with being said date."

"You pay off my debt—I pretend to be devoted to you?"

He eased into a smile this time, slow and sensual. A frizzle of energy lit her belly and she felt a sudden need to swallow.

"Seems more than fair," said Nate.

"Seems like a version of the oldest profession," she muttered.

Clearly not softly enough. "I'm not asking you to sleep with me, Saskia," he said.

"Stop," she said, her cheeks feeling like little spots of heat. "Now you're just gushing."

His laughter was soft, a low chuckle. And then he leant back in his chair, watched and waited.

A pretend boyfriend. A date to a wedding. No more red envelopes. No more reminders of Stu or his letter. The time and the means to get back to renovating the first place she'd ever rightfully called home.

"For the sake of argument," she said, "would you change your mind if I told you *this* is what it would take?"

She threw out the hefty figure that covered Stu's debt only, which she knew to the nearest cent, and he didn't even blanch. Maybe if he'd flickered an eyelid, lost a little colour in that healthy face, or if his long fingers had gripped a napkin in despair that would have been the end of it. But for his complete lack of reaction she might as well have been asking for a tenner for the cab home.

And from one heartbeat to the next she considered his offer.

Seven months she'd been living under the weight of it. Seven long months of driving a banged-up car, of trawling online sales to replace every piece of electrical equipment she *needed* to make a living. Of taking menacing late-night phone calls from debt collectors, legal threats, her mortgage squeezing tighter and tighter. Of being romantically stagnate… None of the debt was her fault, but she was too bone-deep humiliated to do anything but absorb it.

Nate watched, bluer than blue eyes taking in her every breath. The guy was smart, gorgeous, clearly better than well-off. He wasn't going into this thing desperate or despairing. He was doing a deal with all the cool of a business decision. Why couldn't she do the same?

"Do we have ourselves a deal?"

"I get the feeling I'm going to regret this…" she muttered, then held out a hand. He took it and she felt a frisson of heat and something else—electricity, perhaps—shooting up her arm.

Then Nate said, "Who knows? Maybe I'll be the time of your life?"

And with that came a big wallop of charm so bright she had to blink against such brightness.

It occurred to her belatedly that while she'd thought she'd

had him on the ropes, distracting him with talk of infographics and ice-skating, he'd actually been in charge the entire time.

She waited till the buffet of charm subsided, before saying, "Who on earth filled your head with *that* rubbish?"

"Three sisters. All of whom you're going to meet Sunday week at my mother's house."

On that note their dinner arrived: steaming pasta piled high with glistening red sauce, pungent with Italian herbs. The homemade bread oozing with butter. And for the first time ever at Mamma Rita's Saskia lost her appetite.

After dinner—as always, Saskia insisted on going Dutch which, considering the amount he was about to lay down for her services, might have been a tad redundant—Nate walked her through the restaurant and outside where the breeze was brisk, the final notes of winter trying one last stir.

"Where are you parked?" asked Nate, pressing a hand to Saskia's lower back.

She actually felt the warmth of him through her top.

"I'll walk you to your car."

"I walked. I don't live far." She'd planned on walking back too, only now she could afford transport. "I'll grab a cab."

One nod, then Nate looked across the busy street and with a determined wave hailed a cab. He opened the back door for her and she leaned in to give her Brunswick address to the cabbie.

She stood to say *goodbye,* or *thanks,* or *see you soon,* or whatever a girl was meant to say to her new faux-boyfriend.

"It was a pleasure meeting you, Saskia Bloom," Nate said, taking the decision out of her hands.

She placed her hand in his to find it enveloped in his strong, steady grip. "We'll see, Nate Mackenzie," she said.

Nate's laughter was low—a rumble that slid down her arm and faded into the darkness. Leaving them looking into one another's eyes. Hands still held. Two strangers who had just made a deal to pretend to be more.

Saskia moved in for a goodnight kiss on the cheek…right as Nate let go and pulled away.

Oh, God. He'd meant to give her a handshake while she'd—*argh!*

Saskia saw the moment Nate knew it, and as blood rushed from every extremity to land hard and fast on her cheeks a smile tugged at the corner of Nate's mouth.

She opened her mouth to say… Well, she didn't get a chance to say anything, as Nate's hand slid to her waist and he pulled her close.

His blue eyes were shadowed, the street light creating a halo around his dark blond hair. He looked cool, steely, all greys and blues. And yet his touch was hot, as if a furnace burned just below the surface.

His nostrils flared as he moved in slowly, giving her time to call a halt.

But in the face of all that heat and strength, the scent of man, and after seven long months with a wiry, snoring, biscuitoholic dog her only male companionship, she wasn't going anywhere.

A small smile kicked at the corner of his sensual mouth and then, easy as you please, he brushed his lips lightly across hers.

When she didn't push him away, or knee him, he pulled her closer still, shooting sparks of awareness all over her body. Then, with another soft, tantalising press of his lips, he teased her, drawing out the kiss until her lips parted on a sigh.

He didn't waste a second, his tongue tracing her teeth before sweeping inside her mouth. She gripped his jacket as, arching against his hands, into his heat and hardness, pleasure tugged at her belly before pooling lower.

The cold night air pressed in on her back as his heat burned her front. Heat won, pouring through her as the kiss slid into something deeper. Nate fisted his hands in the back of her top and Saskia rose to her toes, sinking completely into the kiss, into him.

As she began to feel drugged, hot and flaky, nearing the edge of control, Nate pulled back.

When she finally found her breath, Saskia asked, "What was *that* for?"

"Credibility."

She glanced up the street to find a few late night stragglers looking in shop windows and ignoring them completely. "I reckon the cabbie's convinced."

Nate laughed, the sound reverberating through her still pulsing body. "So am I, to be honest. A hell of a lot more than I was five minutes ago."

Saskia blinked up into Nate's hooded eyes. When she licked her lips his grip tightened, and Saskia could feel her pulse *whumping* all over her body as her heat levels ramped up in preparation for more...

Then Nate neatly pulled away, making sure she was steady before he let her go completely. She wasn't. Steady. She was wondering if she'd bitten off more than she could chew.

Hands now in pockets, all that latent heat trapped behind a wall of cool, Nate said, "Six weeks and a bit. And a wedding." As if she might need some kind of warning.

You kissed me! She ached to throw it back at him, but she'd been all too willing to let him.

"And debts paid off," she said instead, getting the feeling it would become some kind of mantra in the weeks to come. "And if you decide to be helpful and tell me about your dating life, I'll be all ears."

"Sweetheart, I'd pay double what you asked *not* to have to talk." He held the back door of the cab as she slid inside. "I'll call you soon."

Saskia nodded, and as the cab drove away she couldn't help but look back, to find him standing on the footpath, watching her too. Tall, broad, hair gleaming under the lamplight.

She lifted a finger to her mouth, which still tingled from the attention of his wonderful mouth.

There goes a man I could forgive for snapping my carrots, she thought. *And probably a lot worse.*

CHAPTER THREE

NATE RAN TWO hands over his face, trying to get some blood flowing to his brain. He was working more than ever; the number of emails bouncing into his inbox every minute proved it.

Ignoring them as best he could, he concentrated on the contract on his desk. Bamford Smythe, the "gaming guy" whose start-up company BamBam Games Gabe had discovered, had signed an exclusivity agreement with BonAventure, and now they were in the process of nutting out the finer details of the capital investment.

Smythe was pessimistic, pedantic and paranoid that everyone was trying to steal his ideas. Thankfully he was also brilliant. Nate just had to keep him on a short leash—which was turning out to be akin to lassoing a Tasmanian devil.

A knock at the door and a glance at the watch strapped to his wrist told Nate that it was three already. *Dammit.*

Rubbing a hand up the back of his neck, he called, "Come in."

The door was opened tentatively, followed by a head poking around the door. "Hiya."

"Saskia."

After their date he'd emailed her with a half-dozen questions—basic stats about age, family, schooling. Then she'd called, suggesting they get together for a "get to know one another" in a "pretend we've had a half-dozen dates" kind of way. He'd told her to make an appointment, hoping she might waver. Alas, she wasn't easily swayed.

Nate waved her in with one hand and finished annotating with the other. "Won't be a sec," he said, glancing up as she sauntered in. But his hands stopped midscrawl when he saw what she was wearing.

Her hair was tucked beneath the same fedora from her online profile picture, her legs were swimming in wide calf-skimming pants that looked like they'd been cut from a Hessian sack, sandals were tied up over her ankles, and she wore a brown cardigan she near got lost in, and a scarf long enough that a lesser woman would have stooped under its weight.

A thread of tension shot through him, landing with a twitch at the corner of his right eye as he considered what his family would be expecting. Certainly not this gamine creature who looked as if she might start sprouting poetry or drawing in chalk on his office floor.

What had he been thinking?

She shot him a quick smile as she took a curious tour about the room, her wide eyes shadowed beneath her hat, her lips soft and pink. The memory of how they'd felt beneath his own hit him and hit him hard—her gentle heat, her soft sighs, her sweet response that had licked at something deep inside him. Okay, so he'd been thinking of kissing her from nearly the moment he'd sat down.

She unhooked a satchel from her shoulder and dumped it unceremoniously on the sleek cream leather couch on one side of the room, bending over to rummage through it, giving him a nice view of a pretty fine backside. She might be slight, but he'd felt enough curves as she'd pressed into him to give any red-blooded man pause.

"Gotcha!" she said, standing upright, her profile lit with a happy little smile.

Contentment, he thought again, feeling something akin to

envy at her easy pleasure. At how he'd barely swiped his mouth across hers before she'd started trembling.

He ran a hand up the back of his head several times to get his brain into gear. It was fine. Under other circumstances their unexpected chemistry might be a hindrance, but in this case it would help make them convincing.

And the deal was a good one. Saskia seemed cluey—the kind of person who just got on with things. She didn't seem demanding, or clingy, or prone to tears and pouts. The antithesis of his sisters, in fact.

His tension eased. A little.

She caught his eye, then waved a couple of folders at him before throwing them onto the coffee table, where his assistant had earlier left an assortment of nibbles for their meeting, and moving his way.

"Your desk is so neat!" she said as she moved to perch on the edge of the black chair on the other side of his desk. The chair that had made Gabe look so big only a few days before made Saskia look like some kind of waif. "How do you know where anything is?"

"It's where it's meant to be."

Her mouth twisted sideways. Then she shrugged. "What are you working on?" she asked, pitching forward. The whirls of lace beneath her cardigan scooped low, giving him a glimpse of the sweet rise of the flesh within.

"Contracts," he said, endeavouring to keep his eyes on hers even as his body reacted viscerally, remembering how she'd felt in his arms—warm, soft, all woman. "New gaming company."

"Which one?"

He hesitated, old habits dying hard.

"I'll know them," she promised, misunderstanding his silence. Then, pointing at her chest, said, "Maths degree, remember? Nerd girl."

She looked so expectant, which only made him clam up more. It was a spontaneous reaction, brought on by years spent with women and their need to ask questions, to talk, to pry, to get to the heart of every damn matter. The more they wanted, the less he had to give.

He saw the moment she realised it. Her eyes widened and her lips pursed into a small O. "You're not going to tell me, are you? Is it confidential? No? Okay. But what will I say if anyone asks me about your work? That you keep a tidy desk?"

He laughed before he'd even felt it coming.

If nothing else, he liked her. Honesty and decency shone through the quirkiness. And even beyond the signs of attraction that had led him to email her in the first place aside, their kiss had been natural, raw, effortless. And wanted. By both sides. This *could* work.

"BamBam Games," he said.

Her eyes widened, her mouth twisting as she gave a long, low drawn-out, *"Reeeeally?"*

All that lovely cocky certainly was swept away. "Problem?"

"Not necessarily. Bamford Smythe is a genius. He's going to change the world." Under her breath she added, "Or destroy it from the inside of a cave somewhere."

Nate cricked his neck. "You know the guy?"

"*Of* him. Lissy, my business partner, did some work for him once. The logos and icons on his website are her work."

Nate clicked over to BamBam's website for a quick reminder. It was slick, cool, with an aura of hipster that Bam-Bam…*Bamford* had never given off in person. Now he knew why.

Then he realised Saskia was still talking.

"…and M&M'S. The guy is spookily addicted to M&M'S. So good luck!"

"Right. Thanks."

"Finish your thought and then we can get started," said Saskia, pressing herself to her feet, ridding herself of her long cardigan and tossing it towards the couch.

When she rounded his desk and headed to the wall of windows in only a lumpy lace tank, the beige pants and bondage sandals, Nate found himself watching her walk. Relaxed, easy, a neat little sway to her hips.

Not a mote of self-awareness about the woman—as if it didn't occur to her he might be paying such close attention. That from his angle the afternoon sun sluiced through the window making the buildings glow gold and rendering her lightweight pants all but see-through.

Her silhouette showed off lean legs, gently curving hips and a round, high backside. He curled his hands into his palms till the nails bit deep. Despite the test kiss, she wasn't his to touch. It hadn't been part of the deal.

Her hands went to that waist and she stretched out her shoulders, as if opening to the sun. His blood rushed every which way but loose.

"Shall we do this?" Nate said, his voice gruff.

Saskia turned and he waved a hand to the couch.

Saskia picked out a strawberry before unwinding and kicking off her shoes, taking off her hat, ruffling her hands through her kinky dark hair. Then she sat in one corner, leaving the length to him, one foot under her backside, the other curling its toes into the thick white rug.

She made it look so…comfortable. He wasn't sure he'd ever had anyone barefoot in his office before. He was pretty sure he liked it.

"So?" she said.

"You called this meeting, Miss Bloom," said Nate as he took the other corner. "You have the floor."

"Miss Bloom, is it? Well, then, we are all business."

Her gaze dropped to his mouth, her lips closing around the red fruit. Then, with a soft sigh, she picked up the two neat leatherbound folders with leather ties from the coffee table and handed one to him.

"Flash," said Nate, amazed that his tongue worked when it felt as if it was tied in knots.

"Stationery addiction." She waved a hurry up hand, practically bouncing in her seat as she waited for him to pull out whatever was inside. "I know it's a little more than we agreed to but I'm a sucker for a new project. There's nothing like it—blank paper, freshly sharpened pencils. Anything's possible."

"Before real life gets in the way?"

She shrugged, as if she was still convinced one day things really could work out as she hoped they might. An optimist was Saskia. With Pollyanna tendencies. Nate made a note to remember that.

He opened his folder to find his emailed questions, only she'd expanded them to include a slew of small details, rich details—the kind of details and funny stories people tended to discover about one another on the first few dates. And his were all filled in.

"You researched me," he said, eyes widening as he read on. School subjects, overseas trips, friends past and present, sports played, prizes won, legs broken and a full list of companies he'd invested in, complete with links to interviews he'd given to financial magazines and websites.

"Don't get too excited. I do this for a living, remember. I just found what was out there."

"I'm not sure *excited* is quite the right word." He looked up to find her nibbling at her lower lip.

"I've overstepped the mark, haven't I? *Argh!* Lissy calls it my Puppy Syndrome."

She held up her paws and panted and Nate's blood rushed south with such speed he had to grip the couch.

"But I just like being helpful. Here, give it back. We can start over. Pretend it never existed."

Was she kidding? She'd just saved him *hours.* In Nate's world that made her akin to the perfect woman.

He pulled his dossier out of reach and looked down at hers, gripped in her hot little hand. He found himself...not excited, exactly, but intrigued as to what was contained therein. "Swap."

She blinked, her lashes jerking against her cheeks, then did as she was told.

Nate opened the first page, speed-reading past schooling—state run. Tertiary education—scholarships. Work—applied mathematics with government agencies, before she'd moved on to build her own business—research with a bent towards the statistical.

He slowed when he hit her favourite books, movies, TV shows, as a tumble of odd and wonderful nuances meshed together to form a picture of not just a set of sultry eyes and kissable lips but a woman. *The Princess Bride* nestled alongside *Aliens* and *The Breakfast Club,* Ray Bradbury butted up against Sophie Kinsella and John le Carré. And a litany of real-life adventures flew before his eyes.

Compared with him, she'd lived three lifetimes.

"You've really eaten live witchetty grubs? And—" he glanced down "—you were an extra on *The Hobbit?*"

A smile hooked the corner of her lips, soft pink and warm. "All of the above. They taste better warm. Like nuts. Witchetty grubs, I mean. Not Hobbits," she corrected.

Laughing, Nate said, "Who knew statistics could be so much fun?"

That just lit her up—eyes bright, smile wide, cheeks pink, she glowed like a touch-lamp on level one. He wondered what it would take to light her up all the way.

Clearing his throat, he closed the folder.

Just in time for her to add, "My dad was a maths professor, so we lived in university housing, holidayed on campus. He never left his rooms if he could help it, while I'd sneak out and find people to talk to about things other than chaos theory. To ask about dinosaurs and rainbows and France. Being a university, there were always people happy to oblige. I found there's always potential to learn something new. You only have to ask. So I never say no to possibility."

"Never?"

That earned him a sassy grin. One he felt right deep down inside.

"What was your father like?" she asked. "Was he a lot like you?"

"A good deal." *Worked a lot, took responsibility seriously, blue eyes that laughed easily.*

"How did he and your mother meet?" Her chin rested on her knee, her eyes the picture of innocence. But she'd forgotten, he had three sisters. Her nugget about her own father suddenly made perfect sense. She wanted to get inside his head. He almost felt sorry for her that she was going to waste her time trying.

Nate said, "If it's not in the dossier let's consider it extraneous to the project."

Thwarted, she twisted her mouth.

"So," he said. "Tell me something about me."

"You're testing me?" she said, sitting straighter.

"If you can't pull it off what good are you to me?"

"Fine," she said, crossing her legs on the couch, eyes burning into him, bright with challenge. "Bring it on."

"Favourite colour?"

"Blue." She looked around his white, silver and pale blue office and said, "But you'd have to be colour blind to miss that. Pick up your game, Mackenzie. You're dealing with a pro." She crossed her arms beneath her small breasts, pressing them up, creating swells above the neckline of her top.

"Pets?" he said, his eyes lifting to stick to hers.

She snorted out a laugh. "I'd bet my life savings that you're not home enough to keep a cactus alive, much less a goldfish."

Considering he'd wire-transferred *those* life savings into her bank account only a couple of days before, he knew that wasn't much. But she was right. "You?"

"A dog."

"Really?"

"You don't like dogs?"

"I like them just fine. So long as someone else is in charge of feeding, washing, walking, cleaning up after them. What kind of dog? Please tell me it's not the kind that fits in a handbag."

"Ha! He's an Airedale named Ernest. He belonged to an ex who thought he was going to be the next Hemingway. Turned out he was more opportunist than writer—he left Ernest behind as payment for the TV and stereo he took in his place."

"Ever get them back?"

She shrugged as if it didn't matter. But he was a master of body language, knowing when to attack a deal and when to take a breath, and by the hunch of Saskia's small shoulders it mattered.

"Charming," said Nate, his tone belying his sudden desire to find out the guy's name and hang him from a balcony till he coughed up the goods.

"I came out with the better end of the deal."

"Good dog?"

"Sheds like nobody's business, has a wonky ear, will take a man down for an Oreo. But he's never gonna steal my TV."

Finding it hard to reconcile the woman before him being involved with the kind of man who could do that kind of thing, he moved on. "Family?"

She rolled her eyes. "You're a middle child—older sister, younger twin sisters."

"A psychologist's dream."

"I'm an only child, remember, so get in line."

He laughed and settled back in his corner of the couch. She settled back in hers. *Game on,* her smile said as she spoke. "Your mother is still about. Your father died when you were fifteen. A day before your fifteenth birthday, in fact."

Nate's throat closed over at that last part—a small fact he usually left out, as if it was one intimacy too far. But he'd brought up the subject of family. He'd asked for it.

She opened her mouth as if to say more, but he quelled her

with a look. Then she brought her knees to her chest and snuggled in against the cushions as if she belonged there.

"Women?" Nate asked, even while he wondered instead about this woman, about the kind of men she normally dated. No doubt men with goatees and sandals swarmed around her in droves. Unless she preferred her men clean-cut in suits.

"Your tastes run to brunettes," she said, curling a lock of her own brown hair around a finger, "mostly. Though there have been blondes and the occasional redhead."

"I'm an equal opportunity date."

A flicker of a smile, then, "No serious girlfriend that I could find." That got him a pair of raised eyebrows, meaning *fill in the blanks, please.*

Instead he went with, "Until now."

When her brow furrowed, her sweet mouth turning down, he nodded towards her and saw the moment she got his meaning. Pink rose up the soft column of her neck.

"Though we haven't really touched on that as yet. Are we that serious?" he asked, watching as the pink moved north to land in her cheeks. His palms warmed, as if he could feel the heavy beat of her blood from there. "Or just messing about?"

"A little serious," she said, but only after licking her lips. "Or what would be the point?"

Once his eyes had landed on her mouth there they stayed. And this time, as the memory of how she'd tasted, how she'd opened up to him and kissed him with such easy release came back to him, it did so with a great hot thud. "There's something to be said for messing about."

"Nate," she said. Her lips opened as she said his name.

"Yes, Saskia?"

"Maybe we should talk about the kiss."

With that, his eyes slid back to hers. When it came to his "feelings," *talk* was a four letter word. But if she wanted to describe, in any kind of detail, the kiss, then who was he to stop her? "Talk away."

She carefully put her feet back on the floor, as if needing to ground herself. "What I'd like to talk about is limits."

"Limits."

"Requirements and…restrictions."

God, she looked so earnest he couldn't help but grin. "My hand may brush your hip but must move no higher than your waist? Kissing allowed, but no under-clothes action?"

Her resultant stare was understandably flat.

"We're both grown-ups, Saskia. You know what I want. I know what you want. I think so long as we both get what we want the boundaries can be fluid."

She breathed in long and deep, and he felt himself breathing right along with her.

"So, kissing…" she said, her voice husky as all get out.

"Needn't be off the table. Unless *you* want it to be."

Did she? He'd live if she put a kibosh on it, but he found himself going very still as he awaited her answer.

A few long moments later she sat up straighter, shook her hair from her face and with a small shrug said, "Never say never."

That's my girl.

"So whatever happens…"

"…happens."

"Till the wedding."

"Right." Nate jerked a little at the fact that she'd been the one to say it. Then he shifted closer. "No point knowing about one another's childhood pets if basic chemistry isn't believable."

She sat stock-still, as if they'd been forced together by a fateful turn of Spin the Bottle. She frowned at his smile, which only made him smile all the more.

"What's so funny?" she asked, her voice husky, giving her away.

"You."

"If the thought of kissing me is *that* funny, maybe we ought to cut our losses right now."

"Sweetheart, the thought of kissing you is out there now, like a flashing red light right in the middle of my forehead. I can't stop thinking about it. As far as I know there's only one way to fix that."

"Right…" she said.

He moved closer again, till his thigh touched hers. Her bare feet curled into the couch. Her scent shifted in the air around him—soft, natural, making his nostrils flare and his blood pump so hard through his body he could hear it behind his ears.

He slid a hand into her hair, the softness spilling over his fingers. He turned her head till she was looking at him head-on, to find her lashes at half-mast, her eyes darkened with anticipation. Not a flicker of light was to be found in their bottomless brown depths.

He leaned towards her and smiled as she did the same, till her breath washed across his mouth, hot and ready.

Her chest lifted and fell quickly, as if her breath was getting away from her.

And then he pressed his lips to hers.

Such sweetness, sweeter than he'd even anticipated, as he fed her slow, aching, gentle kisses. And then there was her taste. He'd somehow forgotten that part; the lush, wholesome taste of her that was familiar and unique all at once. Her small hands lifted to grip his shirt. Soft sighs escaped her hot lips.

As her tongue slid across the seam of his mouth his brain turned to wild red mist. He returned in kind, their tongues dancing, chasing, creating the most delicious friction, and wave upon wave of heat rained through him.

Her arms wound around him and her body lifted to his, as if she couldn't get close enough. He felt trembling, though it couldn't possibly have been *him*.

When he wound his hand deeper through her hair, tugging it back, she opened to him as if she'd been unlocked, and all that sweetness was swept aside beneath the flood of heat that erupted between them. Her sweet, hot mouth was like a drug, pulling him under. When one bare foot ran down his leg it was all he could do not to come then and there.

Needing air, he moved his mouth to her jaw, to her sweet neck. God, she tasted like cupcakes with butter icing—sweet and decadent all at once. He slid a hand up the curve of her hip, then beneath her top to her waist. Her mouth opened on an intake of breath as he found skin. Such warmth, such satisfying softness.

When he circled his thumb beneath her ribs she writhed beneath his touch. Hell, the woman was all response. She made his blood pump too fast through his body, until kissing didn't seem like nearly enough—

He heard the phone ring in the outer office and remembered where he was: the company he owned was humming uncompromisingly on the other side of an unlocked door.

He pulled away with less haste than he'd intended. His hands took their time to leave her body. His mouth trailed back to hers for one last taste.

Then, using every ounce of self-control he was able to muster, he leaned back on the chair, as far away from this strangely compelling creature as possible.

Her eyes fluttered open and she stared at the ceiling, her legs twisted, her clothes askew. "Well," she said. "I'm sure glad we got that sorted."

He laughed. Then laughed some more. And thanked his lucky stars he'd found Saskia Bloom.

She pulled herself up to sit, ran a hand through her hair and only managed to make it look more rumpled. Provocative little thing, she was. He wondered if she had a clue.

"We done for today?" he asked.

"And then some," she said, shooting him a smile still lazy with lust.

While Saskia heaved herself from the couch Nate glanced at his watch, saw it wasn't even four. He had hours of work left to do, but knew without a doubt he'd be lucky if his concentration strayed above fifty percent capacity.

"I'll walk you to the lift," said Nate, picking up the dossiers.

"Keep them," she said, grabbing her hat, her cardigan, her huge bag. She was soon lost inside them again. "Some light reading for you. And if you feel like I've missed out any important details in your file feel free to jot down notes."

Nate pressed his thumb into his temple.

"You do that a lot," Saskia said. "Rub your temples. Or run a hand up the back of your hair. I wonder if you keep your hair so short so you don't tear it out."

She sat to retie her shoes, crossing the straps over her small ankles. When Nate found himself staring, imagining himself dropping to his knees and undoing them all over again, he distracted himself with his dossier, opening it to a page labelled "Identifying Marks."

Hello!

"You have a tattoo?" His eyes drifted over her lean form, landing on spots that might sport a tattoo of some breadth. "I should probably know what it is. And where."

Her eyes narrowed slightly. Then she set her feet on the floor, walked around the table. She turned away from him and lifted the loose top to reveal a small tattoo at the top of her shoulderblade.

A swathe of her hair was in the way, giving him no choice but to move it to one side. Her skin contracted under his touch. His gut tightened at her reaction. And the urge to kiss her, right there, came with a powerful push.

"A rose?" he said.

"My mother's name. Rosetta, actually. She was holidaying from Spain when she met Dad."

Her mother—who had died giving birth to her.

Losing his father had been horrific. Life-altering. Every dynamic in his life had shifted overnight. Even while Nate's mother drove him crazy he couldn't imagine not having her in his life. And yet Saskia Bloom, was, for all intents and purposes, an orphan of the world.

She lifted her shoulder away from his touch and let her hair fall back to her shoulder. "Not what you expected?"

"I was all prepared for a Chinese symbol for…something."

She rolled her eyes at him. "Unless I know a language intimately I'm not letting some biker with a needle write it on my skin."

A biker? Who *was* this woman?

Whoever she was, she was smiling at his shock. And in a flash he saw fearlessness behind that smile. A girl without a mother. A woman without a father. Alone in the world. And yet she was bright with effervescence, drive, gumption, humour and fearlessness. Looking into her lovely brown eyes for a moment, he could feel wind in his hair, the sun on his face as he left the world behind.

"Do you have any tattoos?"

He blinked, came back to the real world. "I do not."

"Want one?" She leaned forward, grabbed her bag and a grape, popping it into her mouth, where she rolled it around with her tongue before her teeth sank into it with an audible pop.

"I'm sorry?"

"A tattoo," she said, licking grape juice from the corner of her lip. "I know a guy who'd just love to get a hold of all that nice clean skin of yours."

"You think I have nice skin?" he asked, his voice dropping a notch.

Her head tilted, as if she was considering answering. Fearlessness won. "I think you could do with some ruffling."

"Ruffling?"

"You're so clean-cut. Even your background is pristine. No parking tickets."

"I fob those off on my driver."

She laughed—a husky sound he felt as a tightening in his gut.

"No restraining orders."

All she got for that was a raised eyebrow.

"I've taken out three. Two of them against the same guy."

Again Nate found himself sideswiped by the sudden urge to tear a complete stranger limb from limb. Time to call this meeting over. He pointed a hand towards the door. She hitched her bag and headed that way.

"You've clearly been dating the wrong kind of men."

"Tell me about it."

He got a knowing grin over her shoulder for his efforts.

"I certainly have a type."

"What type is that?" he asked.

She thought about it a moment, her mouth twisting. "Men with needs I can't help but fulfil."

He gripped the doorjamb to stop himself from fulfilling his own rabid need to dive his hands into her hair and ravish that mouth till she could no longer feel her legs.

When she hitched up her big bag again Nate slid a finger under the strap and tucked it over his own shoulder instead. Then he stepped through the door, dragged in a lungful of air filled with the scent of cleaning product and money and inside his head started listing stock exchange codes…alphabetically.

"Anyway, that's by the by," she said, smiling at his assistant as they passed by her desk. "I'm with you now."

Nate's assistant raised her eyebrows at Nate, who mouthed, *Get back to work.*

They walked companionably towards the lift. Nate nodded to any staff they passed, each one casting glances at Saskia, no doubt desperate to know who she was. He wondered if any thought they might be a couple.

"How about you?" Saskia added as they hit the vast foyer.

Nate put a hand to her back to ease her around the scattered chairs. "Do I intend to fulfil your needs?"

"Identifying marks," she said with a smile.

For once it didn't seem too much to ask. "I have an appendix surgery scar and a birthmark on my inner thigh."

"Shape?" she asked.

Her eyes slanted to his lap. Nate had never had cause to wonder about death by abstinence, but in that moment he was beginning to imagine the possibility.

"Texas," he lied, and thanked God when her eyes shot back to his. "Kidding. It's roundish."

"I guess I'll have to take your word for it."

The lift door opened and she held out her hand. He was half a second from taking it, using it to drag her in for one last kiss, before he realised she wanted her bag back.

He waited till the lift was clear bar anyone but her before saying, "So, next is my family lunch on Sunday."

Her shoulders flicked to her ears. "Nervous?"

"Not a bit," he said as the lift doors began to close.

"Liar." She grinned.

His laughter continued even when he was looking at nothing but the lift door.

"So that's your date?"

Nate turned to find Gabe leaning against the reception counter, his eyes on the lift. Nate made a beeline for his office, not keen on having this conversation in the foyer.

"Not what I expected," said Gabe, falling into step.

"What's wrong with her?"

"Not a thing. She just seemed…normal."

And even though Nate knew he was being baited he rose to it before he could stop himself. "What she is is cool. And funny. And mouthy." He pictured her standing in his window, hands on her hips, opened to the city view, the light shining through her clothes. "But mostly she's got this level of contentment I never even knew was possible."

"I think Nate has a crush on his pretend girlfriend."

Nate shook his head. "What Nate *has* is a contract to read for the third time."

Gabe winked at Nate's assistant, who giggled like a school-girl, then stopped in the office doorway, grinning. Nate pointed a sharp finger at his business partner. "*You're* going to Vegas."

"I am?" Gabe asked, standing straighter, his dark eyes shining with thoughts of treasure.

"With Bamford Smythe."

"The hell I am."

"He likes M&M'S. You're taking him to Vegas and getting him a private tour of M&M'S World. And when he's nice and high on chocolate fumes we're getting the nitty-gritty of this damn deal locked in."

Nate could feel Gabe reacting to being told what to do. They were equal partners, after all. Had been since day dot. But after Gabe had disappeared all those years before, leaving Nate to pick up the slack, Nate had never used the "You Owe Me" card. Not once.

Even while he couldn't believe it himself, Nate felt it shimmer on the air between them now. Over Bamford Smythe.

For reasons of his own Gabe took it on the chin, striding off towards his own office to make it so.

Nate thumbed his temple and stalked behind his desk. When he realised what he was doing he pulled his thumb away. If even Saskia, whom he'd met twice, had noticed his stress, he needed to take a break. And soon.

Or he was seriously going to crack.

CHAPTER FOUR

SASKIA STOOD LEANING against Nate's car—a glam silver sporty number that would have gone down well in a Bond movie—on the street outside a massive Stonnington Drive home. Its three clear storeys of gabled roofs and picture windows gave its imposing façade familial warmth, even while the shade of a hundred-year-old oak in the front yard added to the late winter chill.

No wonder Nate had looked so relieved when he'd picked her up at her door a half-hour before. The poor love had probably expected her to turn up in hemp and a hat. Instead she'd gone for a little lipgloss, a little more mascara, fitted jeans, layered tops, a tailored jacket and ballet flats. He didn't need to know the frilly scarf that hung to her knees was a million years old, second-hand and homemade.

"What a beautiful home," said Saskia, having a Molly-Ringwald-in-a-John-Hughes-movie moment.

"Mmm."

His tight response was so chilly she literally shivered. She gave herself a good mental shake. Then a physical one—stomping her feet and shaking the blood back into her hands.

"What are you doing?" Nate asked, his voice tight, his whole body stiff as a board.

"Trying to relax."

"Try harder."

He was serious. Which only made her laugh. Hard. Giving the butterflies in her belly a good workout.

"Enough already! How do you *expect* me to act? Faking it in front of a guy's family is hardly a common occurrence in my life. How about yours?"

His sensuous mouth grew flat, his stare much the same.

"Didn't think so. Because *you're* not doing such a bang-up job of looking like a guy who likes a girl enough to bring her home."

His jaw clenched so hard he was in danger of breaking a tooth.

"Here." She reached for the top button of his shirt, and stopped when he flinched.

Jeez, the guy was so wound up that if she flicked lint off his jacket he'd probably self-combust. She spared a glance at the door of the beautiful-looking home perched at the end of the perfect white gravel drive and wondered for a second what she'd let herself in for.

But it was too late for all that now.

She'd promised to help, so she'd help. She'd be such a great amount of help he'd never forget it. Maybe he'd be so touched he'd open up a little, give her fodder for her study.

"May I?" she asked, hand hovering an inch from his chest.

"May you what?"

"Ruffle you up a little."

"For what purpose?"

"For the purpose of making you look like a man on a date, not like an undertaker."

He breathed deep, his chest lifting till the weave of his luxurious woollen jacket brushed the hairs of her arms, creating skitters of...*something* all the way to her elbows.

His gaze finally left the house to connect with hers. The tangle of blue was enough to take her breath clean away.

"Ruffle away."

She purposely lowered her gaze from his eyes, not quite

sure what to do with the warmth that seemed to have seeped in there from one second to the next.

Instead she focused on the top button of his shirt and slid the button through the hole. When she saw he wore a crisp white T-shirt underneath—heck, even that had been ironed—she undid another button, and another. Her fingers slid beneath the collar as she softened out the starch. The backs of her knuckles brushed against the warm cotton of his T, and the beat of his heart didn't feel so steady.

Because of what he was about to try to pull on his family, she told herself. For the less than steady beat of hers her excuse was less clear.

"You have a good reason for doing this, right?" she asked, flicking her gaze to his to find him watching her fingers. Intently. She pulled them away, tucked them into the back pockets of her jeans. "For lying to them. For their own good? For yours? For world peace?"

He sniffed out a laugh and looked up at her from beneath his unfairly long lashes. "What if I told you the reason was less altruistic?"

What if? she thought. But she didn't have any qualms. She trusted his heart was in the right place. Or right enough. Her allegiance was with him.

She slid her hand into the crook of his arm, her hip bumping his companionably. "Come on, lover. Let's go make them believe."

She pushed away from the car and escorted him up the path, the scent of roses clear and lush on the crisp air. He unhooked his arm and slid it around her waist. She did the same to him, his body heat pressing in on her.

They walked side by side up the steps. Eyes on the big white double doors with a great lion's head knocker snarling back at them.

Saskia looked at Nate, waited till he looked back at her and made sure he was listening. "This thing between us is new, so if I don't know something I'll say so. All you have to do is throw me a hot glance every now and then. Undress me with your eyes a little. They'll eat it up."

He stared at her for longer than was comfortable.

"What?"

"Hell, Saskia," he said, his voice a growl as he ran a hand up the back of his hair—a move she was already familiar with.

She slipped her hand into his and gave it a squeeze.

Then when he looked down at her in question she lifted onto her toes and kissed his cheek. The rasp of his stubble tickled her lips. The scent of him slipped down the back of her throat.

Which was when she might have hummed.

The flicker of heat that sparked to life in Nate's eyes made her sure of it.

He lifted a hand to her cheek, his thumb running slowly across her cheekbone before his fingers disappeared into her hair. Brow furrowing, his eyes roved over her face, leaving *her* eyes to rove over his. And what a face. Noble nose, thunderbolt eyes, lips just made for kissing. She'd tried not to remember just how good they were at that particular job, but it was an impossibility.

So much so that, when his tongue darted out to wet his lips and he bent towards her Saskia was so filled with anticipation she began to tremble.

Which was when the front door swung open, letting out a shaft of golden lamplight and noisy chatter.

Nate blinked as if coming to from a spell, then as one they looked up as a gorgeous blonde rolled her eyes at them.

"Get a room!" said she.

"Faith," Nate growled, taking Saskia's hand and holding it tight behind his back as if he was her human shield.

"Nate," said Faith. "And you must be this new girl we've heard about. Glad to meet you."

"Saskia Bloom," said Saskia, but Nate had her in such a tight grip she was forced to hold out her left hand.

Faith took it, laughed, shook her head, then waved a hand to usher them in.

She bounded off, her long blonde hair swinging, but Nate kept Saskia back a moment.

"Thank you," he said, his breath brushing her ear as he leaned in close.

"I haven't done anything yet."

"Yes," he said, waiting till her eyes found his. "You have."

Then he stepped back so that his eyes could slide down her form, touching on her neck, her wrist, her thighs, before slowly meandering back to her eyes.

"Now, let's do this," he said, then winked—quick, brief, but potent—before he led her into his family home.

And while Saskia tried to get over the fact that gorgeous Nate Mackenzie had just well and truly undressed her with his eyes, for a brief moment she imagined running. Far, far away.

But Saskia was a stayer. Through thick and thin. You could take her stuff, call her names, ignore her through an entire childhood and still she'd never leave you. It was her defining quality. And, no matter that Nate Mackenzie was proving to be a trickier proposition than she had at first realised, she wouldn't let him down.

In fact he'd be so impressed with her awesome girlfriendness he'd open up and give her all the research material she'd need to do her piece. To write her love formula. To understand why some people found love every day of the week and others didn't no matter how hard they tried and how much they wanted it.

She just had to keep one step ahead of him or she'd turn into a puddle of lust on his mother's floor.

Saskia's coping mechanism was sophisticated, but surrounded by the females of the Mackenzie clan, her nerves were just about shot after less than an hour.

They were all gorgeous, like Nate. His mother effortlessly

charming, like Nate. So it should have occurred sooner that Nate's family would be as sharp as he too. As dogged. As tricky.

Interweaving questions about her, and Nate, and her and Nate, with talk of current affairs, reality TV, school friends she'd never heard of, keeping her spinning in circles till her inner ear was on its last legs.

"You're not his usual type," the one with the silver earrings—Faith—threw into the middle of an argument about the men in *True Blood*.

Nate's older sister, Jasmine, pinched Faith till she cried out, and then looked sweetly at Saskia. "What she meant was you're a real woman."

Hope rolled her eyes and stuck a rum ball in her mouth.

Saskia said, "As opposed to an imaginary one?"

Faith stopped rubbing at the pink mark on her arm, her eyes cutting to Saskia before she barked out a round of raucous laughter. "You know something we don't?"

Sure do, Saskia thought. But she just shrugged, looked Faith right in her big blue eyes, and said, "Nothing I'd share even upon threat of torture."

Faith grinned. "I like you. Stick around, if you can manage it."

They *liked* her, Saskia thought, making her wonder how they treated those they were less than keen on.

Later, cradling a much-needed coffee, she found a quiet corner, slowly sweeping her eyes over the great room at the rear of the house. The women were chatting, gossiping, sharing their favourite books. Saskia felt herself watching them as if they were the subject of a nature documentary: Women of the Mackenziegeti...

The guys were watching footy—black and white versus blue. Jasmine's twin boys had turned the dining table into a fort. Nate, on the other hand, was nowhere to be seen.

The whole afternoon he'd kept himself apart, just beyond the edges of conversations, hiding behind a coffee, or a beer, or a nephew. While she'd watched them all in open-mouthed awe.

Growing up, she'd wondered what it might be like to have a big family, and watching the shifting dynamic of this group of people, the vibrant debate beneath the warm glow of the beautiful home, she felt a twinge of envy. A kick of regret. And her first pang of guilt.

She was on Nate's team. No matter what. But she wasn't sure Nate's team was doing the right thing. Whatever it was that kept him at arm's length from his family, that made him think he had to lie to them rather than have it out with them, he certainly didn't seem willing, or able, to fix it himself. The only outcome she could see was that one day he'd be so far removed *he'd* be the one feeling he was on the outside looking in.

She found him in the kitchen, which was surprisingly devoid of action. He was swishing his thumb over his phone, brow furrowed. His other thumb was pressed into his temple, and not for the first time that day.

Her fingers itched to rub it for him. To make everything all better.

Instead she leant in the doorway and said, "Howdy, stranger."

Nate looked up from his phone, expecting his mother, or one of his sisters. He could never seem to go five minutes without one of them tracking him down, making sure he was happy, that he hadn't disappeared.

When he saw it was Saskia, her soft mouth smiling indulgently, the clench in his stomach unwound and he put his phone away. "Howdy yourself."

"I wasn't sure if you trusted me to hold my own or if you'd just gone into hiding."

"We can go any time you please."

"I'm fine. Honestly. They worship you."

"Hmm."

She leant a hip against the sink. "Poor Nate. To be so adored."

He turned to face her. "Want to swap?"

She glanced back to the swing door, where noise poured through the fretwork above. All too late he remembered she had no-one.

"Saskia—" he said.

But Faith bustled into the kitchen before he had the chance to take it back.

"Nate? Oh, there you are," said Faith. "Half-time. Game-time."

"No."

"What's game-time?" Saskia asked.

Nate held out a hand to shield Saskia, but it was too late. Faith took her by the hand and dragged her through the door. "You're going to love this."

Faith shot him one last look before the door swung closed—and a grin that left him worried for Saskia's safety.

Knowing he'd left her alone too long already, he followed, leaning quietly in the doorway of the lounge, arms crossed, nursing a beer as his family went about their loud business around him.

Usually he took these moments to think about work, to disappear inside his head and pull himself away from all that energy. And history. And emotion so thick it clogged his throat.

This time they seemed to have forgotten to try to include him, now that they had a new victim to bat about, so he let his eyes rove over the scene, taking it in.

Hope was midargument with her girlfriend Tanya—a wholefoods wholesaler—about which kinds of flour were gluten-free and which weren't. Poor Tanya, so earnest, while Hope's eyes were gleaming, her Mackenzie genes loving every second of the battle.

Faith pinched her fiancée on the backside on her way to the kitchen with an empty salad bowl.

Jasmine was washing down the face of a toddler with a baby wipe, calling him back when he tried to leave before he was picture-perfect. Nate found himself wincing in sympathy.

The Mackenzie women were tough, uncompromising. He felt a small, swift kick of pride at the fact, considering where they'd all been twenty years before—the way it might have all turned out so differently if he hadn't done everything to make sure they felt safe, secure, loved, protected. If he hadn't given every ounce of his heart and soul, and then a little more, to give them the safety net from which to leap out into the world.

He breathed into the void it had left inside him, the vacuum where empathy and love had resided once upon a time.

"Look what you did."

Nate turned to find his mother behind him, her eyes taking in the same picture as his. He stood straighter. "I think you'll find they're all yours."

"We're all *ours*," she corrected, leaning her head on his shoulder as she gave him a squeeze. Then she lifted her head to look him in the eye as she said, "I like your girl."

It was on the tip of his tongue to say, *She's not mine,* but he caught himself in time, offering a small smile before he brought his beer to his mouth for a swig.

"You know what I like most?"

"What's that?" he asked, pretty sure it wouldn't be the same thing *he* liked best.

"She makes you laugh."

"I laugh plenty."

She laughed at his frown. "You *smile* plenty. A mere glint in those eyes of yours and you can get away with anything. But it's always taken a lot to make you laugh. And today you seem more...relaxed." She tugged at the open collar of his shirt. "It suits you." Then, after a long, slow breath in and out, she said, "Have I told you lately how proud I am of you?"

"Half an hour ago."

"Okay, then." She gave him a kiss on the cheek before heading into the fray with a tray of cookies.

Leaving Nate with the same sense of ruefulness he always felt when they looked him in the eye and said, *Well done, you.* As if it was as important to them as it was to him that he'd made something of himself. And just like that he felt a pressure headache building behind his left eye.

It was why he gravitated to women whose appeal was surface-deep. Who wanted him for surface reasons. His money, his touch, his charm. Replenishable resources all.

He glanced across at Saskia. Her motivations for being with him were simpler still, and yet far more complicated than he'd envisaged. Because compared with his usual dates, Saskia was...*real*.

Reality was scrappy. It was dirty, hard, complicated. It asked everything of a man and then some. His father dying young, leaving him with four women in varying stages of grief to look after, had given him a closer dose of "real" than he ever wanted to encounter again.

And yet here this woman was, real from the top of her wavy hair to the tips of her now bare feet and her short fingernails—a couple bitten to the quick. He looked at her slight figure. The way her right foot rubbed up and down the back of her left calf as if it might bring forth inspiration as she stared at the scrap of paper in her hand. She was first off the mark in Faith's game of high-speed half-time charades.

Saskia looked up at him then. Two little lines showed above her brow, her bottom lip was disappearing and reappearing from between her teeth. There was entreaty in her gaze.

He tilted his head in question. She flicked the paper in her hand. Two weeks they'd known one another, yet there was a shorthand there. An understanding that he couldn't remember having with another woman.

Maybe it was because there was no pressure. No demands.

Maybe it was because they both knew it was a few weeks, a wedding. And out.

But even while he felt his twin sisters' eyes swing to him at the same time, even while he knew they were smart enough to know there was something different about this one, Nate put down his drink and went to her.

And he had to admit, as Saskia threw herself into the game with gusto and a complete lack of success, that those twenty odd minutes were some of the most fun he could remember having in that house in a really long time.

After lunch Nate found Saskia looking out of the French windows in the library, watching Jasmine's husband and kids playing chase in the backyard. She was leaning over the back of a couch, her backside pointing nicely his way.

He shoved his hands into his jeans pockets.

"Come here often?" he asked.

She came to with a start, as if from a million miles away, before a smile stretched across her face—which had his eyes zeroing in on her mouth, making him wonder when they could get the hell out of there.

"That the best line you've got?"

"I don't usually need any."

"I don't doubt it."

He might have let it go if not for the fact that her cheeks had turned a completely gorgeous shade of pink. "Really?" he drawled.

She rolled her eyes. "Like you don't *know* you're gorgeous."

She said it so matter-of-factly, and yet her admission slid through him like a wave of heat. And when her eyes connected with his awareness surrounded them like a net—heavy, tight, confining.

"So…" Saskia said, moving around the couch, clapping her hands together and using them as a shield.

Interesting. She was aware of him. She liked the look of

him. Clearly. And now she was trying to pretend it didn't mean anything.

Maybe it didn't, he thought.

Then again, maybe it could.

It was four weeks till the wedding, and he didn't see why they couldn't enjoy themselves in the meantime.

He took a step her way and her eyes flickered.

He took another step until she'd backed herself against a bookshelf.

He put a hand on the shelf above her shoulder and very much enjoyed her shiver at his near touch. The rise of her chest, the way her lips fell apart. At a noise in the hall Saskia's gaze cut sideways, leaving him room to whisper against her ear, "We want them to walk in on this."

"We do?" she asked. Then, as an afterthought, "Walk in on what?"

"This."

He pushed her hair aside and kissed the soft skin of her neck. Her scent poured into him like pure pheromones. He pressed himself against her. Thank God she pressed back. Her hands lifted to his shoulders, where they gripped for dear life.

"Nobody's watching," she said, her voice a rasp as he trailed kisses along her jaw.

He dropped a kiss on the corner of her sweet mouth. "Then consider it practice."

Her hand slid to curl around the back of his neck, her hips rocking against his and making him see stars.

Even while his body screamed at him never, ever to stop, he knew things were fast getting out of hand. Having his sisters and mother believe he was attracted to Saskia was one thing. Being caught with the evidence in his pants was quite another.

"Come with me," he said, grabbing her by the hand and dragging her after him without waiting for a response.

Up the stairs he went, two by two, with her keeping up behind. They hit the hall and he just kept on walking till they reached his old bedroom.

With his hand on the doorknob, he balked, realising how long it had been since he'd been inside. Years. Decades. Maybe his mother had turned it into a guest room. Or an after-hours seniors disco. Hell, he hoped so. And he hoped not. It had been his refuge during the hardest years of his life.

He pushed the door open and as the ghosts of his past rose up and surrounded him with such complexity, such vividness, he felt himself sway.

Saskia shot past him. "Oh, my God," she said, laughter in her voice. "Is this your room?"

His eyes on hers, Nate felt his tension ease back a notch. He crossed his arms across his chest and looked right on back. "Not anymore."

"No? You *don't* live at home still, then? I know you own like a million houses, but we never did touch on which one you live in…"

"Funny girl."

Saskia gave him a curtsey before taking a slow turn about his room, forcing Nate to follow. The room was big; the bed-spread, dark wood furnishings and the nautical wallpaper were the same as they'd been the day he'd left.

When Saskia ran a finger and thumb softly down the sail of an elegant three-foot yacht on the chest at the end of the bed, Nate said, "Dad and I made that one when I was about eleven."

She shot him a glance. Then she kept walking, as if it *wasn't* as important an admission as it clearly was. "Good with your hands. Nice to know. Anything else? For the dossier, of course."

A good listener was Saskia, he warned himself, and an eager one, with an ulterior motive. And yet still he said, "He made the small ones downstairs too—the ones in the bottles. It was his favourite hobby. Mine too. Until it wasn't."

Her eyes swept back to him—open, warm, filled with un-derstanding. "Nate…" she said, her voice husky.

His thumb pressed against his temple.

"You need to stop doing that," she said, pulling his hand away.

"It helps."

"Find another way. How do you relax?"

"I don't. I work." He glanced up at her, then admitted, "Occasionally…yoga."

"Hardcore relaxing. Does it work?"

"If I let it. Which isn't as often as I ought."

"Why not?"

"I have…responsibilities."

"As do we all."

"I have over a hundred employees who depend on me. Every decision I make affects them. And their families." Nate lifted a hand to the back of his neck, but stopped it there. How had that happened? He'd walked away from being responsible for four souls only to become responsible for hundreds. No wonder he never took a day off.

"Nate, you might be their boss, but they are, each and every one, responsible for themselves. On the other hand, I wonder if you spend near as much time worrying about yourself."

Saskia's eyes roved over him then. Over his eyes, which he knew looked as tired as he felt. Over his shoulders, making him feel the tightness of the muscles bunched therein.

She reached out, slid her small hand back into his and led him to the bed. There she pressed him down with gentle hands at his shoulders.

He sat, bouncing on the mattress, looking up at her.

She smiled a little before lifting her hands to run them through his hair. Front to back. Her fingers sliding across his scalp with perfect pressure. The touch was such a surprise he blinked at her. Speechless.

"I've been wanting to do this since I first saw your picture," she murmured.

Then, when her hands moved back through his hair, against

the grain, tugging slightly against the short strands, he closed his eyes with the complete and unexpected pleasure of it.

When her thumbs moved to his temples, making small insistent circles right where he needed it most, he groaned at the sweetness. He put his hands behind him on the bed and gave himself over to the sensation. The pure relief.

There they stayed for seconds, minutes, until the constant pressure that lived inside his head ebbed away.

As her hands moved to his neck, kneading at the tight muscles bunched there, her knees bumped his. He opened them to let her closer.

When her outer thighs brushed his inner thighs all relaxation fled in a heartbeat, leaving him unquestionably aware of himself. And her.

His eyes swept open to find her watching herself work, concentrating, with those little lines above her nose. Clueless to the fact that she was trapped between his legs. That her breasts were at his eye level. That she was so close that when he breathed deep through his nose he could smell her—not just her shampoo and her soap but her skin. Her heat. Her essence.

When he lifted his hands to her waist she flinched with surprise.

She braced her hands against his shoulders. Her eyes flickered to his. Her next breath in was deep, her breath out lush. As if she'd known that touching him would lead to this.

Her thumb grazed the outside of his neck, sending shivers through him. Leaving him baffled that this lean, soft, down-to-earth woman could create such anticipation, such rich layers of desire coursing through him with no more than a brush of her thumb.

And surrender in her eyes.

One hand at the back of his neck, she leant down and pressed her lips to his.

He knew to expect sweetness, to expect warmth, to expect

her clean, honest taste. What he got was a jolt of heat so thick that the blood rush to his head near wiped out all thought.

He wrapped his arms around her to drink it in. All of it. All of her.

She opened her mouth to him, sank her body against his, and all that softness and warmth pulsed through him till he wrapped his arms so tight about her there wasn't a millimetre of daylight between them.

Yet for all that he wasn't close enough. He wanted to be inside her. Inside that heat and ease and peace and sweetness. He wanted her with a level of need he hadn't felt in a long time.

As if she felt it too she pressed nearer again, till he tipped back, taking her with him. Her hair tickled his cheeks. Her mouth was like a siren song, drowning him till his brain was a haze of red, and sex, and Saskia.

Nate rolled until he was on top. Looking down at her. The dark waves of her hair splayed out on the plaid bedspread, her cheeks flushed, her lips dark pink and plump, her eyes drunk with desire.

"Having flashbacks?" she asked, her voice husky, her fingers playing with the back of his hair. "I'm betting I'm not the first girl you've made out with in this room."

She was right. And she had him so hot he felt seventeen all over again. Clumsy, desperate, on the verge of losing himself in her.

He shifted till his hardness was nestled against her and her eyes fluttered closed.

He ran his thumb down her cheekbone, traced her bottom lip, the dip in her chin. "Would you have played hooky with me back then?"

"Not on your life. I was a good girl. Classic only child. Pleaser. Head in a textbook. Didn't have my first real kiss till uni. Marty Grantham. Chemistry major."

Again Nate found himself gripped with a desire to track this Marty down and clock him one, even though by the lift of her mouth her memories of *him* were all good. Sweet kid she must have been then. All alone. The desire to protect her, from that and more, swelled from some place deep down inside him and landed like a punch to the solar plexus.

Saskia didn't leave him any time to dissect it as she slid a hand to his neck and dragged his mouth to hers.

Desire, and thunder, and instinct pounded him from all directions. Nate tried to keep his head, but pleasure ripped through him as her tongue slid neat and clean along the edge of his bottom lip, before she found his tongue and traced it with hers. Lust pressed against the outer edges of his skin, raw and rabid, nothing neat about it.

Her hands were clawing his back, his backside. Her leg around his waist, then her hand moved between them, cradling his length. A groan spilled from his mouth as he pressed into her hand, relishing the feel of her around him, beneath him.

A fog of rich red lust swarmed over him, wiping out everything in its path. Control, order—gone. Screw it. Screw it all. All he wanted was this. Her. *Now.*

"Nate? Are you in there?"

He heard his mother's voice all too late.

"Oh," she said, before the bedroom door slammed shut.

Nate could only hope she was on the other side of it.

The fog cleared faster than it had come over him, leaving the world around him crystal-clear. The glow of the old red lamp on his bedside table, the dust on the edges of the shelf with books and old toys leaning against them, the grain of the bedspread digging into his wrists.

He glanced down at Saskia to find she'd slapped a hand over her eyes, her body tensed like a rubber band stretched to its outer limit.

His mother's muffled voice came through the door, "Just letting you know Jasmine and the boys are heading off if you want to say goodbye."

"We'll be down in a minute!"

"Rightio," said his mother, with more than a little laughter tingeing her voice before her footsteps padded away.

"Saskia," Nate said, once he was sure they were alone.

"Mmm-hmm?" she said, trying to roll up in a ball beneath him.

"She's gone."

"Mmm-hmm."

A smile creased his face. "Just because you couldn't see her didn't mean she couldn't see you." He peeled her hand from her eyes to find them wide and wild. Heat still lingered. More than lingered. It pounded behind her eyes. Drenched with desire.

He felt the same pounding rekindle deep in his belly. The drumbeat of lust was pulsing through him as she shifted beneath him, the length of him cradled between her legs.

He heard Jasmine and the boys downstairs, calling out their goodbyes, and he bit out a curse as he pushed himself away from Saskia. He heard the bed creak and turned to find her straightening up, running a hand over her bed-tousled hair. She might as well give up. She looked well-tumbled.

If only, Nate thought, then caught himself, thanking heaven they'd only gone as far as a kiss. If what they'd been doing before his mother had stumbled upon them could be called something so simple as a kiss.

"Hell," he said, running a hand over his face.

"Think they'll believe we're an item?" said Saskia, her bright eyes cutting to his.

And he realised she didn't think it as funny as he did. In fact she looked more than a little shell-shocked.

Swearing again, Nate moved to sit beside her, taking care not to touch. Touching this woman was not a smart idea unless he intended following through.

"That's not what that was," he said, running a hand up the back of his head. "That wasn't for their benefit."

She sucked in a quick breath. "I know."

"Do you?" he asked, reaching out to tuck a kink of dark

hair behind her ear. So he couldn't help himself. That much was fast becoming clear.

Saskia looked from one eye to the other and Nate felt himself being weighed and measured. And for a man who'd long since been in a position where nobody who judged him could find him lacking it was a strange sensation indeed.

"I really wanted to kiss you," she said simply.

"I wanted you to kiss me."

"I got that feeling."

"Did you, now?" he asked, a smile easing across his face. The relaxing of his shoulders showed him how tense he'd been. How concerned that he'd been that he'd stuffed things up royally. How much he wanted things to continue…until the wedding. "Though as I recall, heavy petting on my childhood bed wasn't part of the original deal."

"Let's call that a renegotiation."

At that Nate laughed so loud his sides hurt. "You're a savvy operator, Saskia Bloom. In fact, why don't you work for me?"

"I like being the boss."

"Mmm, woman after my own heart."

When he'd first come upon that picture of a girl in a hat with big, sultry eyes, he'd struggled to believe them the same species. Yet the more he got to know her the more alike it seemed they were. Stubborn, determined, captains of their own destiny. Equals in very many ways.

Then with a saucy little lift of her shoulder Saskia was up, heading for the door. "The sooner we face them, the sooner the mortification will be over and done with."

"You're one hell of a woman, Saskia Bloom," said Nate as he took her hand.

"Don't you forget it."

CHAPTER FIVE

"You what?" Lissy yelled to be heard over the sound of The Cave's house band who'd just started up a grunge version of "Perhaps, Perhaps, Perhaps."

"I kissed him," Saskia said, the words no easier to spit out second time around. *Stupid, stupid, stupid,* she sang inside her head along with the chorus.

"I thought you already had. By the cab. And at his office."

"I kissed him again."

"Where?"

"At his family home. In his childhood bedroom, with sailing ships and baseball mitts watching over us."

"You hussy."

"It's worse. My hand was on his…you know…when his mum walked in on us."

Lissy clutched her stomach and fell to the couch they had staked out at The Cave a couple of hours earlier.

"We barely spoke on the way home after," Saskia said. "Then he walked me to the door, kissed me on the cheek and went on home."

Between clutches at breath Lissy managed to get out, "You tell me I crave dysfunctional relationships—but, honey, you take the cake."

"It's not dysfunctional. We're merely…renegotiating the terms of our mutually beneficial agreement."

"Until one day I come to work and find a tie hanging on the door handle."

"No," Saskia said. Then, "I don't think so anyway. We haven't discussed it."

"You haven't *discussed* sex? Sweetie, I saw his photo. You don't *discuss* sleeping with that. You just hold on tight and enjoy the ride."

Saskia swallowed. Not that it helped. The lump in her throat at the thought of holding on to Nate Mackenzie, enjoying Nate Mackenzie, *riding* Nate Mackenzie was immovable. Much like the guy himself. From the second he'd come knocking on her email he'd loomed larger than life.

"It was right that we stopped," Saskia said, straightening.

"Why on earth?" Lissy asked, eyes large with astonishment.

"It's complicated."

"It's really not. You take your clothes off, kiss a bit, he puts his—"

"It's temporary!" Saskia nearly shouted to stop Lissy from putting any more images in her head. Nate was *naked* in there now, as it was, his hot-as-a-furnace skin all glistening with sweat.

"The majority of love affairs are temporary, hon. But that doesn't diminish the possibility the next one might become something more."

"Nate's not a possibility, Lis. He's like the door of a bank safe—all big and hard and shiny and tempting, but impossible to get through."

"Knock harder. There's treasure behind that there door."

"Maybe," Saskia said, frowning.

"Oh, sweetie," Lissy said, dragging herself upright to hold Saskia by both cheeks. "You should see the mope you have on right now. You *like* the guy. For real. He might be pretending, but you're not."

Saskia shook her head—hopelessly, as it turned out, because Lissy had caught the arm of a busboy and was flirting him into getting fresh drinks for them. Leaving Saskia to think it out on her own.

She *liked* kissing him. The man had skill.

She *liked* pretending to like him. It was great fun. A caper.

She *liked* Nate too. How could she not? Every layer she managed to laboriously shave away only revealed more to like beneath. And more to make her certain that despite the perfect appearance, Nate was a true fixer-upper.

But… But what if she found the combination to unlock that door and discovered that his odds at finding and keeping love were as dim as the rest of the poor saps out there? What hope did she have then?

"Good God," Lissy uttered. "No wonder you felt him up all over."

Saskia blinked and turned to Lissy who was staring at some point over Saskia's shoulder.

"Here's a love formula for you: those shoulders plus that jaw line plus oh, my word, what a mouth equals…"

Right as the band hit a crescendo of onerous drums, screeching sax and groaning bass guitar, Saskia turned and found herself looking right at Nate Mackenzie. He was making his way through the crowded bar, smiling at anyone who caught his eye, and unless it was a coincidence of the highest degree he was looking for *her*.

"What's he doing here?" Lissy asked.

"I have no idea. I mean, I might have mentioned I'd be here tonight, but not in an invitation sort of way."

"Well, he's here—and he's not alone."

Saskia dragged her eyes away long enough to see Nate had an entourage: a collection of shiny gorgeous things behind him, looking around The Cave, taking in the mismatched chairs, the shabby old couches covered in faded velvet, the bad acoustics, the scratched and dented vintage signage.

Her heart thundered against her ribs as her hand went to her hair, which had long since gone to curl. Her skinny jeans, ballet flats and layered tanks were good only for dancing, which meant the likelihood was that her mascara had long since turned to panda eyes.

Finally Nate's eyes found hers. Dark, blue, intense. She lifted a hand and his mouth cocked into a half smile which was different from the one he bestowed upon strangers. Gentler, warmer—just for her.

I know this man, she thought in a moment of wonder. *I've kissed this man. I'd really like to kiss him again.*

Lissy was right, she thought with a groan. She wasn't one hundred percent pretending any more.

She stood as he approached; his suit was slick, he had not a hair out of place, and a beam of light slanted across his stunning face, picking out his sensuous mouth and sapphire eyes.

"Beautiful," she thought. But before she could catch the word she realised she'd said it out loud.

Nate's brow furrowed a moment, before it cleared and he laughed. As if hearing such a thing from her wasn't so unexpected after all.

A loud clearing of the throat brought Saskia's attention back to Lissy who was standing behind her batting her lashes. At Nate and at the big guy behind Nate.

"Nate," said Saskia, "this is Lissy—my friend and business partner. Lissy Carmichael—Nate Mackenzie."

"Love Formula research bunny, in the flesh," Lissy said, giving Nate's hand a good shake.

Saskia could have killed Lissy. She honest to goodness could have thrown her over the back of the chair for that one. But she had to put on a smile as Nate's gaze skewed back to her.

"Better than a lab rat," she said.

Thankfully that brought laughter which hummed across her chest. "True."

Lissy sat down and grinned over her cocktail.

"More trouble than she's worth?" Nate murmured against her cheek as he moved around behind her.

"You have no idea."

When his entourage appeared through the haze like a band of perfection Nate placed a hand in the small of her back. There was no suppressing her shiver at his light touch. Nate must have felt it. Might even have liked it, if the way he spread his fingers around to her waist was anything to go by.

"Saskia Bloom, this is Gabe Hamilton—*my* friend and business partner."

Saskia looked up—and up—and shook hands with about the biggest man she'd ever seen.

"Pleasure," said Gabe in a voice as deep as he was tall. He drew an attractive blonde to his side. "This is Paige. My fiancée."

"Next up we have Mae and Clint," Nate said. "It's they we have to thank for bringing us together."

Mae grinned, while Clint seemed to be eyeing the bar.

Saskia waved them all onto ottomans and over-soft couches—whatever they could drag around the low coffee table.

Clint's backside had barely hit a chair before Mae put in her drinks order. "After the dinner we've just had I need a big blue jug of something sweet and deadly."

Saskia watched all this with Nate's hot fingers pressed against her side, pretty much diffusing everything else to about half strength.

Then he said, "And you know Bamford, of course."

Well, *that* got Saskia's attention. She hadn't even noticed the scruffy-looking gaming king off to the side of the group, sorting the M&M'S in his palm into colour blocks and then throwing them into his mouth one at a time. From the corner of her mouth, to Nate she said, "I've never met him before."

Nate's eyes widened. "But didn't you say—"

"I said Lissy had worked on his website for a time. And found him a pain in the ass."

Nate ran a hand up the back of his head and swore, looking comically pained.

She asked, "What's going on here?"

"Celebratory dinner. The contract's all done, signed. Thanks, in part, to you."

"Me?"

"You inspired us to schlep him over to M&M'S World in Vegas and it put him over the edge."

"Wow. I mean…that's fabulous! Do I get a finder's fee?"

His blue eyes snagged on hers and his hand dropped from the back of his head. His mouth kicked up into a half smile. Anxiety forgotten. *It's a gift,* she thought, glowing from the inside out.

"What you get," Nate said, eyes smiling deep into hers, making her glow brighter still, "is the chance to help a friend get through this night before he strangles someone."

A friend, Saskia thought, liking the term a whole lot. Because the truth was she really liked Nate Mackenzie. And friendship sounded a heck of a lot less disastrous than the feelings buzzing around inside her, starting where his hand rested possessively against her hip.

"Dinner was atrocious," he continued. "The guy complained so much, about everything, I kept waiting for the chef to appear from the kitchen brandishing a carving knife. Then I remembered you'd be here. You were my last hope to make this evening anything other than horrendous."

Wow. If Saskia hadn't already thought herself on the other side of pretending, the guy had just pushed her over the edge with a neat little shove.

She widened her eyes in warning that he owed her for this, and moved to meet Bamford Smythe.

"I'm Saskia Bloom of SassyStats. My colleague did some work on your website last year. It's an honour to finally meet you."

Bamford blinked as if coming to from another plane. And

then Saskia saw the direction of his gaze. His eyes were all on Lissy, who was bouncing in the chair as the band lurched into a grunge version of "Dancing Queen."

"Did you meet Lissy? She did the graphics for your site," Saskia said, nice and loud.

Lissy looked up from her cocktail, her straw caught between her teeth. She saw who Saskia was talking to and her jaw dropped. Saskia knew her friend well enough to see the war going on behind her pale green eyes. Bamford was famously difficult, but in their circles he was a god. And behind the scruff he was actually pretty cute.

Lissy twirled the straw with her tongue, just once around the rim of her glass, before she pressed to her feet and thrust herself deep inside the computer genius's personal space. Saskia sent out a word of prayer on Bamford Smythe's behalf.

Saskia turned back to Nate with a smile. "How's that?"

Nate leaned in so as to be heard. "You are my very own little miracle-worker. Again."

"It's a knack."

"One of these days I'm going to have to repay you for all this. Properly."

Right, Saskia thought, flinching on the inside. And there she'd been *liking* the guy, because somehow she'd let herself forget that at the heart of everything was the deal. Not friendship, not desire. Just a tenuous arrangement that stretched between now and a wedding.

"It's fine," she said, waving it away. "Happy to help. Puppy Dog–syndrome, remember?"

Nate angled his head, motioning to a quieter part of the bar. Saskia grabbed her beanie, scarf and her ex-army jacket with all its helpful pockets for money, ID and the like, hooking it over her arm, extricating herself from the group and following.

"Drink?" he asked, once they'd found themselves a spot at the end of the bar.

"Ta," she said, perching on a bar stool.

"I'm paying," he shot back as she reached into a pocket.

"Honestly, you don't have to. Thanks to you, for the first time in months I have money to burn, remember?" There, now he'd been reminded too.

"Doesn't mean a guy can't buy you a drink," he said. "I insist."

She'd never had a guy *insist* before. Pretend to, sure. But the difference was clear. And it felt unexpectedly nice. *Oh, what the heck?* she thought, and let him.

"In recompense I'll even let you take notes just this once," he said with a smile as the bartender slid them each a bottle of imported beer. "'Nate's Moves on a Date.'"

"So we're on a date all of a sudden, are we?" she asked, spinning to press her back against the bar and then taking a swig.

"You tell me."

She opened her mouth to tell him…something. But nothing came out. At the directness of his gaze, the glimmer of something warm and relaxed deep in his eyes, his nearness, his latent heat, her tummy was twisting and diving too much for a quick comeback to occur to her.

"Some place you've got here," he said, letting her off the hook with a grin that offered a now-you-see-it-now-you-don't dimple. "It's got a good energy."

Saskia leant her elbows back on the soft old wood and sighed. "I love it. Since uni it's been my home away from home. They make the fattest, crunchiest fries on the planet and their coffee is the absolute best."

"Only one thing—"

"What's with the music?" she finished.

They both listened a moment to the dissonance of deep rumbling ABBA lyrics cranking out of the fuzzy old speakers.

"I think it's meant to be ironic."

"It's terrible."

Saskia's teeth gripped the lip of her beer bottle as she grinned. "Yeah, I know. It's a dive. The lead guitarist in the band is the owner's nephew to whom he pays nothing. But I think there'd be a revolt if it ever changed."

Nate's eyes dipped to her mouth, then to her throat as she took a swig and swallowed. She tucked a foot onto the long metal footstand running around along the bottom of the bar and held on with all her might.

Nate's eyes remained narrowed in her direction, his fingers tapping on the bar, as if he was deciding whether or not to say what was really on his mind. Then a muscle twitched in his jaw. "I've been meaning to call to thank you for coming to lunch with my family."

"They were convinced?"

"Convinced I don't deserve you."

"I am rather adorable when I want to be."

His mouth kicked at one corner again, but there was no humour in his eyes. Dark clouds had swirled in, taking too strong a hold. His hand lifted and he brushed a knuckle down her cheek. "I think you're rather adorable even when you haven't a clue."

"Nate," she said, in warning, or maybe in entreaty.

Either way, Nate lifted himself from the stool and moved around in front of her slowly, till she was trapped between the man and the bar, the heat of his skin sending her nerves into meltdown.

She tried to tell herself they'd done more than enough renegotiating. That friendship was all she wanted. That she feared the treasure behind the vault doors was too rich even for her.

But then his fingers slid beneath her hair and he bent down till his lips were a whisper away from hers. "I need to kiss you, Saskia. Right now."

And before she knew it he *was* kissing her—as if his life depended on it. Her hands slid up the back of his jacket and her leg twined around his strong calves, till she disappeared into heat, desire and sumptuous sensation.

He pulled her to her feet. Her flat shoes landed on the sticky floor with a thump. And when his mouth moved to her ear, sweeping a shot of breath over the lobe, her knees all but gave out from under her. His arm was at her back, dragging her against his body, and his readiness, his need, had her biting her lip to stop from whimpering.

Then his voice, deep and insistent was at her ear. "I lied. I didn't come here because of Bamford. I have not been able to stop thinking about you since last weekend. About your warmth, your sweetness, your glorious mouth. There's this light inside of you, Saskia Bloom, and all I have to do is touch you and it burns me up right along with it." He lifted away, just enough to take her face in both hands, look deep into her eyes and say, "I want you. And I'm not enough of a gentleman to pretend I don't know you want me too. Let's get the hell out of here."

Saskia's eyes flicked between Nate's, lured by his incessant heat. He wanted her. While her whole body throbbed from wanting him.

Yet a little voice in the back of her head whispered just loud enough to be heard above the rush of blood. He might want her now, but this was not a man who would ever wonder how he lived without her, which was ultimately what she wanted.

She licked her lips, and when he looked like he was coming back for seconds she put a hand to his chest. Fighting the urge to hook her finger through his shirt and lose herself in his kiss. In his everything.

"Nate?" she croaked.

"Yes, Saskia?' he said, his voice not much clearer than hers.

"I'm not sure this is smart."

"Screw *smart*."

Her blood filled with liquid fire, meaning she had to gather every last shred of sanity she could find and said, "I'm not sure I have it in me. I finished high school a year early, I have first-class honours in Applied Mathematics; smart is my fallback position. And I think we *should* fall back."

He fell back not an inch. In fact he might even have pressed a little closer. Close enough that the scent of him filled her nostrils and made her head spin.

She'd told Nate once she *never said never*, but the less fanciful truth was she simply found it hard to say no. And with Nate leaning into her, all hot and male and husky with desire, she'd never wanted to say no less in her entire life.

But from nowhere some kind of latent self-protection mechanism rose out of the mist. "It's not real."

He blinked at her. "You sure as hell feel real to me," he ground out.

"Would your friends agree?" she asked. He looked at her as if she was making no sense. While she felt more sensible in that moment than she had since she'd spied him slinking through the crowd. "I mean, do they know the truth about us?"

He might have flinched, but she couldn't be sure.

"What does it matter?"

"*Do* they?"

He shook his head, as if clearing away cobwebs, before he looked at a point over her shoulder. "Gabe knows."

"And what does he think?"

His eyes shot back to hers. Still hot, still rippling with desire. Only now there was a thread of desperation beneath. "He thinks I'm a fool. He's love struck and out of his head. He's not the man he used to be." He pulled back. Ran a hand through his hair and swore, convincingly.

"So if he knows then Paige knows?" Saskia said, not backing down.

"Probably."

"Mae and Clint too?"

"I don't understand the big deal," Nate said, exasperation tingeing his words. "I'm not going to gather them together and let them know we went home together, if that's your concern."

"It's not." In fact it was the opposite of her concern. His friends assuming he was sleeping with the woman in his life was *normal*. "It's fine that your friends know. Better, actually. Lissy knows. And, like Gabe, she thinks we're crazy. And this…" She touched his chest, felt it heave against her palm, pulled away. "This is probably why. If we take this any further we'll be blurring the lines so much we'd be the only ones who no longer knew the truth."

It was more than she'd meant to reveal about her nascent feelings for the guy, but she was scrambling.

Then Nate had to go and turn his intense blue eyes her way and hit her with, "What if we *weren't* faking it?"

"Nate, don't."

"A date. For real. You and me. We've done dinner. You've met my family. I'm not seeing anyone else, just like we agreed. So what do most women consider a perfect second date? Paintball? Paris?"

"I'm not most women."

"Tell me about it."

He looked so solemn. Hot, a little angry, and a whole lot turned on. But it was the solemnity that made her like him— and want him—even more. With a ferocity that stole her breath clean away.

"We'd date. We'd end up in bed. But to what end?" Saskia asked, her voice gentling.

The heat in his gaze gave her imagination some idea of his answer. But it wasn't the one she was looking for.

"This was all fine in theory, Nate. Getting to hang out with a hot guy for a few weeks and maybe even pretend to be like most women for a bit."

He opened his mouth to say something about that, but she held up a hand in front of his face.

"But the truth is I'd like to meet a guy, date him, meet his family for real, swap keys, move in together, get married, have kids—"

Nate came over all pale and swallowed as if his mouth was filled with sand.

"And there we have it, folks."

"What?"

"You look like you're about to pass out!"

"Do you blame me?" he asked, pacing. "You're three steps from walking me down the aisle—which is exactly the kind of hell I was hoping to avoid in finding a date online."

"Thanks so very much."

The look he shot her was dark. Her heart thumped against her ribs. She was liking the darkness. She needed professional help. "Nate. Honestly. Do you want that? A wife? Calm down!" she said when he started to pale all over again. "Not me, *per se,* but someone? Some day?"

"Are you really saying that if I said that I was all about the 'Australian Dream' you'd come home with me?"

Ignoring his attempt to sidetrack her, Saskia said, "Have you even ever come close?"

The darkness in his eyes deepened. Worse, it cooled. And right there she had her answer.

He might be hot to the touch, but at his core Nate was untouchable. And Saskia had already spent more than half her life desperately doing everything at her disposal to make someone love her, never to be quite sure if he did.

And Lissy's postulations had been right; Saskia did keep repeating the same relationship pattern, over and over. But in that moment, she realised that for all the wrong he'd done her, Stu had changed that.

She'd pretended not to notice that he didn't really love her, that he was using her, because it felt better to have someone in her life than not at all.

Never again. And if that meant steeling her heart against Nate Mackenzie—a man whose very kisses spun her emotions so far out of control she felt like flying—then so be it.

"I like you, Nate." *More than is in any way sensible.* "And once this is over I'd like to look back on our crazy caper with a laugh. I have enough regrets about my past relationships, and I'd rather not feel that way about you."

Even while she could see it physically pained him to do so, he listened. He really did. She had to give him props for that. But what she *wouldn't* give him was her body. Her heart.

"I like you too," he said finally, with a physical effort obvious at admitting even that much. "But I have my reasons for not wanting to go down...*that* route. Good ones."

"I'm listening," Saskia said, softening.

His mouth twitched at that, but the smile didn't reach his eyes. "You women and your need to talk."

Saskia's mouth twisted into a smile. Maybe this was a good thing. Maybe they'd needed this moment to finally find their boundaries. They could go on from here as friends. Funny, though, it didn't feel quite enough this time around.

Nate turned to face the bar, his fingers gripping the edge, his gaze far away. "So what do you suggest we do from here?"

"Maybe we stop renegotiating and stick to the plan?"

"Yeah," he said, propping his head between both hands.

She held out a hand, making sure to keep an arm's distance from the guy. "Deal?"

His eyes slanted to hers. Beautiful, blue and a little bit tortured. Poor love had probably never been turned down for sex before. She steeled herself and even managed to conjure up a smile.

"Deal," he grumbled, taking her hand in his. His heat skittered through her. She knew he felt it too. Struggled to contain it. Whatever it was. But this time he didn't do anything about it. Till he said, "At least you have to let me see you home."

"The two of us? In the back of a cab together? How do you think that'll turn out?"

"Yeah," he said again, his voice a growl.

He downed his beer with three large gulps. Then he shook his head at her.

And after one long last sweep of his hot blue eyes down her

body and back up again, leaving her feeling as if he'd stripped her bare right there in the middle of the bar, he turned and walked away.

Leaving Saskia shaking all over.

Feeling as if she'd won some kind of battle.

And lost it all at the same time.

It was a couple of hours before Nate took a cab back to the office. Another again before he slid behind the wheel of his car and headed home.

As he slowed before a red light he switched on the radio, clicking past Tom Petty singing about bad boys and breaking hearts till he found Duran Duran singing about hunting and hunger, and his mind spun through the hours spent trying to be charming, and gracious, and the perfect host to his new client.

It shouldn't have felt like so much hard work. He'd been to more client dinners, celebrations, parties, all out raves than he could remember. He'd lived them, rocked them, until they'd gone down in legend.

But that night, when Nate had pointed out that Gabe had spent more time talking to Paige than to their star client, the two of them had near come to blows. And it had taken for Gabe to tell Nate to calm the hell down, as Bamford—with Lissy on his lap, hand-feeding him pretzels—was having the time of his life.

The light turned green, and when the car in front didn't pull away instantly Nate's fist landed on the horn. He overtook the first chance he had, the gears shifting hard and fast, the sports car rumbling deep and throaty beneath him.

He was so damn tense, if he didn't do something about it, soon, he'd get into fisticuffs with his best friend. Or tell a client what he really thought of them. Or do something really stupid, like join an online dating site for real.

Taking a corner a little sharper than safe, he eased his foot from the accelerator.

He'd start small. Take a day off. Go fishing. He and his dad had loved fishing. The peacefulness. The contentment. There was that word again, only this time it had context. Was the last time he'd felt content? Could it really have been when he was twelve years old? That had to be fixed.

Problem was, he knew exactly how he wanted to get loose. With Saskia Bloom beneath him. Up against a wall. In the back of a car. So long as she was hot, and naked, and making those sweet gasping sounds she made whenever he kissed her neck.

Saskia, who'd put on the brakes.

The city lights swept across his windscreen in time to the beat.

It made no sense to him why they shouldn't explore that in the short time they had. In fact the natural end to their relationship made taking every advantage of their chemistry seem the most uncomplicated decision possible.

He turned into his street, where large homes nestled behind imposing fences. He pressed the remote to his wrought iron gate, before gliding up the curved drive and pulling to a stop outside his front doors.

He rolled his hands over the leather steering wheel as the car ticked and cooled beneath him.

He was not known for backing down at the first hurdle, and just because he was considering dropping a line in the ocean at some point in the future, didn't mean he'd gone soft.

It was a little under three weeks till the wedding. That gave him twenty days to charm the pants off her. Literally. To show Saskia that a man and a woman could like one another just fine, and could also tear each other apart in bed, and it didn't have to mean anything other than a good time.

He was the best damn negotiator in town, and if he couldn't negotiate that he didn't deserve the title.

Feeling better about things than he had an hour ago, Nate

pulled the key from the ignition, leapt from the car and jogged up the front steps. Whistling "Fame." Or maybe it was "Footloose." Whatever it was it brought a smile to his lips, which had to be a good thing.

CHAPTER SIX

ANOTHER WEEK OR SO went by before Saskia and Nate saw one another again.

He was busy; she was hiding out. Or maybe she was busy and he was hiding out. Either way, Saskia kept herself busy.

With Stu's debts all paid—and, oh, what a liberating feeling it was finally to put that whole sordid business firmly in her rearview mirror!—she had real money in her bank account for the first time in months. Money with which to get back to turning her crumbling little house into a home.

And, like a woman who'd been kept away from chocolate for months, and then been given the key to the Cadbury factory, she might have binged. Just a little.

Furniture. Paint. Fixtures. Tiles. Her house smelled like a hardware store. And she couldn't have been happier!

Spring was a little over two weeks away, and it was pouring outside. Typical of Melbourne's contrary weather. At least it gave Saskia the excuse to start a fire in the brand-new fireplace she'd helped fit the day before. Music played softly through her new wireless speakers. And she switched on a couple of her new lamps: leadlight and ridiculously romantic. She'd fallen in love with them at first sight.

Looking around at the eclectic, bright, functional, vintage pieces mixed in with state-of-the-art electronics, emotion swelled in her throat.

The truth was she couldn't have done it without Nate. For

that—for him—she'd for ever be thankful. As for the fact that she wondered where he was and what he was doing several times a day and dreamed her raunchiest wishes into existence at night…that was something she'd have to hope would fade in good time.

She downed the last of her coffee, covered her usual attire of multi-coloured tights, oversized sweaters and ugg boots with a smock, and was halfway up a ladder in her bedroom when her phone beeped.

It was a message. From Lissy.

Chinese or Indian?

Lissy had been fixing a client's website on site all day and was coming for dinner.

Whatever goes best with scent of paint thinner.

Indian then. See ya about seven.

With Lissy out, Saskia had painted the bedroom earlier that day. The wall above her bed was now dry, so she measured for the picture she'd had leaning against a wall for months. Tape, spirit level, pencil in hand, she measured vertically, horizontally, then stood back and looked at the dot with a view to the wall as a whole. Her tummy gave a happy flutter. Symmetry was a beautiful thing.

Yin and yang. Balance. Not just in art, but in life. In love. She was the active participant in her relationships, drawn to people who were content to be more passive. It made mathematical sense. At least she'd always thought so.

Till Stu.

The taking of all her things had been a pretty proactive thing for him to do. The hurtfulness entirely deliberate. As evidenced by the note he'd left on her kitchen bench. In ten short lines, including three spelling mistakes, he'd taken apart everything she'd done for him and thrown it back in her face like a bucket of acid.

"Emasculating," he'd called her. "Bossy…stubborn…a pain in the ass."

She'd only been trying to help. Believing that was what he'd wanted. What he'd needed. Believing he'd love her for it. If he'd just told her, asked her to back off… She'd probably have been so shocked her brain would have short-circuited.

Had all the men in her life thought that way about her? That she was stifling? Unbending? That she was so used to taking care of herself she didn't know how else to be?

She was still staring at the dot on her wall, the pencil in her mouth, when there came a soft knock at her door.

Cursing softly around the pencil, she rid herself of the smock, washed her hands then, with one final pointless run of her hand over her hair, which was curling madly in the heat of the now roaring fire, she opened the front door with a flourish.

And there stood Nate, a day's worth of stubble covering his hard jaw. A few sparkling drops of rainwater stuck to his short hair. A few more dried on the grey T-shirt stretched across his impressive chest. A casual jacket gripped his broad shoulders and faded jeans clung so lovingly to his thighs she couldn't even allow herself to notice properly for fear she'd start to hyperventilate.

For the first time since she'd known him, he looked…*ruffled*. And, boy, did it suit him. It made him seem more accessible, somehow. Her perverse heart gave a happy little thumpety-thump.

Then Ernest bounded out of nowhere and stuck his nose in Nate's crotch.

"Easy," Nate said, laughing, surprise crinkling his eyes.

"Ernest!" said Saskia, lunging for his collar.

But Nate was down on his knees at that stage, rubbing behind Ernest's the collar in the spot he liked best.

"He must smell these," Nate said, tossing her a small blue

box which—miraculously, considering her lack of dexterity—
she caught.

She stared for several seconds at the box of Oreos. Then at
Nate. Then at wiry Ernest, who was by now staring into the
middle distance, tongue lolling out of the side of his mouth,
back leg slapping against the floor in ecstasy.

"You've done that before," Saskia said.

"I'm a man of hidden depths."

Don't need to tell me, she thought, while trying not to appear as flummoxed as she felt. "Come on, kiddo, you've taken
advantage of the man quite enough." Saskia clicked and Ernest gave Nate's hand one last lick before trotting back into
the lounge room.

"Bossy," said Nate.

After her trip down amnesia lane she felt her eye twitch
at Nate's choice of that particular word. "I find it gets the job
done."

Nate pulled himself to standing, his eyes creasing into a
smile as he said, "Hi."

"Hi," Saskia said back, hating that she had to clear her throat
afterwards. "To what do I owe the pleasure?"

He broke eye contact as he reached down for the dossier
he'd dumped on the floor so he could pat Earnest. "I finally
got around to adding some bits and pieces. Thought you might
like a look."

He held it out. She took it. And *flummoxed* didn't even begin
to name how she felt at that. It was a small miracle.

"Now?"

"Unless you're busy?" He glanced over her shoulder and
she realised she was blocking the entrance as if he was trying
to sell her something.

"No. Nothing that can't wait. Come on in."

He squeezed past, his scent—hot, spicy—washing over
her till she had to grip the door handle for support. And she
couldn't help thinking of the last time she'd seen him, the look

he'd given her, as if it had taken every bit of civility in his arsenal not to throw her over his shoulder and take her back to his cave.

"Coffee?" she asked, her voice husky.

His eyes crinkled again. "Why not?"

She turned towards the kitchen, leaving him to follow, and couldn't deny the little thrill scooting down her spine at the sound of the door shutting softly behind him. "What gave you the sudden urge to dive into shark-infested waters?" she asked, waving the dossier over her shoulder.

"I had some free time."

"So says the man who made me consider keeping smelling salts on my person in case he passed out at the mere mention of anything deep and meaningful."

She switched on her machine, set up a pair of espresso glasses and reached for a pitcher of milk. She came out of the fridge and leapt out of her skin when she found Nate just behind her, his eyes roving over her hair.

When he reached out to her, her wide eyes followed his hand. And just like that she was back in the bar, her heart racing, warmth tugging low in her belly, not able to quite catch her breath. Wondering how she was possibly going to find it in her to deny him a second time...

"You have paint in your hair," he said, pulling forward a strand that was white from root to tip.

Right.

"I'm renovating," she muttered, moving quickly to her new butcher's sink to madly wash out the paint. And to silently yell at herself to *get a grip!*

Nate had agreed to move into a holding pattern. The fact that he was here with the dossier proved it. He was trying to uphold his end of the deal. Perhaps even going the extra mile to "repay" her in other ways, as he'd out-and-out told her he'd wanted to do.

Glancing up from beneath her wet hair, she saw him taking

in the gorgeous new wooden cabinets she'd installed herself, the deep turquoise walls and tiny red tiles, and the old vinyl floor she'd yet to replace, before his bluer than blue eyes landed on her. And her now dripping hair. She tucked it behind her ear.

"New?" he asked.

"As of about three days ago."

"And I can smell paint."

"That was this morning."

"You've had a house full of contractors?" he asked, both eyebrows lifting towards his hairline.

"I did most of it myself."

"*By* yourself?" he asked.

"Mostly. I haven't tackled the electrics, so don't panic. You're safe."

His mouth kicked at one corner. Safe? As if he'd felt unsafe before? Afraid she might jump him at any instant? Maybe he was right to worry. He nearly filled her small kitchen, and catching his scent with every breath was making her head spin.

She gripped the sink and leaned back. "It came to a bit of a standstill after my ex took off with all my stuff, so I've gone a bit crazy this week because it's the first chance I've had to do so in so long."

"I thought you said it was just your TV?" he said, his eyes pinning her to the spot.

"And my surround sound."

"And...?"

She twisted her mouth, wondering if she oughtn't just blow him off, change the subject, flash her boobs, anything not to have to talk about *that*. But he was looking at her in that way he did—interested and protective. As if should Stu be in the room he'd no longer be attached to his man parts. And then there was the fact of the dossier, sitting on her small red Formica kitchen table.

She checked the coffee grounds, then rested her hands on the settings. And in a rush of breath, she admitted, "And my computers, my books, CDs, DVDs, coffee maker, toaster, every piece of furniture. He wiped out my bank balance and took all my shoes. My neighbour saw him back up the truck, and thought we were moving. He left Ernest, a couple of tins of the only brand of dog food that he *doesn't* like, a phone bill in my name that would cripple a small country and backed the truck into my car before disappearing into the sunset."

She turned on the coffee machine so it filled the air with the noise of coffee beans crushing and the delirious scent of the same. When the coffees were made she turned back to find Nate had shoved a hip against the kitchen bench. His thumbs went into the waistband of his jeans, so his hands framed the contents therein.

He said, "Hence the debt?"

"Hence the debt."

Nate looked around again, seeming to see her place with a fresh eye. "Have you tracked him down?"

"Stu? Good God, no." The note he'd left had been more than she could take. "I'm fine now. I have a job that's getting more and more successful, I have a roof over my head, I have a cute sugar daddy—what more do I need?"

Nate's eyes were slanted to her, a frown above his nose—until her meaning dawned and the frown turned into a smile. And then a deep laugh filled her small kitchen, before bouncing around inside the cavity of her chest awhile.

Needing something to do with her hands other than place them on the big man in her kitchen, she shoved a double espresso at him, grabbed her own coffee and the dossier and ducked past him back into the large main room, which was now blistering with heat from the fire. At least she assumed it was the fire. But there was no way she was about to dim it—that would be as good as saying *Is it hot in here or is it just me?*

"The place was barely inhabitable when I bought it," she said, giving him the grand tour. "Decades-old wallpaper dangling off the walls. Holes in the ceiling. A bathroom floor near rotted through. The ultimate fixer-upper."

"And you are a sucker for a new project?" he said, pulling from nowhere a comment she'd made in passing weeks back.

Once again Saskia had to remind herself—just because he looked a little ruffled, and rumpled, and faded, and warm, and cuddly, and was saying nice things about her home, it didn't mean he was any closer to wanting what she wanted from life than he was a few days ago.

"Impressive," he added, finishing his turning circle close enough that she could smell the rain on his clothes. Feel the heat of his skin pressing in on her even more than the fire at her back. He smiled down at her, as if oblivious to the effect he was having. "A woman who can change a lightbulb all on her own."

When, under the effect of all that nearness, the ground felt as if it was tipping under her feet, Saskia blurted, "I can't cook to save my life."

Nate laughed, the sound filling the room. "Good to know."

She led him to the third bedroom, where she'd set up the office. It was cooler in there, and her skin thanked her for the respite from the stuffiness of the rest of the small house.

The desk—a reclaimed wood dining table covered in paint splotches and pen marks and nicks and notches sat in the centre of the room, her chair and computer on one side, which was covered in teetering piles of notes on yellow legal pad paper, with colour-coded notes stuck all over them. To anyone else it probably looked like a disaster waiting to happen, but Saskia knew where every single scrap of paper was. Lissy's computer and chair were on the other side of the huge table, which, incongruously, considering the person who used it, was clean as a whistle.

The rest of the room was all cream paint and raw furnishings. Built-in shelves were filled with rattan baskets found at flea markets; soft-furnished guest chairs held cushions and throws. Sprays of stripped willow in an array of huge vases filled up the far corner. A dog-eared copy of *Catch-22* nestled amongst her other favourite books.

"Great room," Nate said, his eyes skimming too quickly to settle on any one thing. "Love the lighting."

"The original fixtures were hideous—straight out a horror movie. I do believe you're *actually* interested in my renovations. I'd be a little worried if I didn't know better."

Nate's eyes slid back to hers, laughing, vibrant, lit with something she hadn't seen there since she'd known him. "The BonAventure offices were refurbed a couple of years back," he said. "The same decorator did my apartment, and I was so busy at the time I let him go nuts—which is why I live in what looks like the home of a sixty-year-old big game hunter. I worked more closely with him at the office."

"Nate the interior decorator? I'm shocked."

"Gave Gabe a laugh."

"Maybe because he's more manly than you?"

"No argument there," Nate said, which only made him seem manlier still.

Ruffled, rumpled, even a little rugged, she thought, staring at the scuff on his boots, then at the loose thread on the collar of his T-shirt.

A skitter of something new and sweet and just a little frightening trickled down her spine. Shaking it off, she waved a hand at a guest chair which was nudged up against the short end of the table. "Work first, food after?"

"Sounds fair—work?"

"The dossier. You've come to the party on my end of the deal, right?"

He looked at the folder in her hand, then at the guest chair as if it might bite, before lowering his length into it.

Saskia sat in her soft pink bouncy office chair, one foot sliding to rest next to her backside. She twisted back and forth and stuck a pen in her mouth. The mixed feelings that came with having Nate so close edged away as she slid into work mode.

Popping her vintage glasses onto the end of her nose, she grabbed the dossier and opened it to the first page. But she'd already filled that out.

"What are you wearing?" Nate asked.

Saskia went cross-eyed as she looked at the incongruously big glasses perched on her fine nose. "They're for reading."

"They look like you nicked them from your grandfather."

"Never met either. And they're vintage." She went to turn the next page when Nate interrupted again, "What's that?"

Sighing, she took off her glasses and glanced at her monitor and a big hot pink rectangle with *Electric Dreams: Finding Love in the Digital Age* scrawled across the top in curly girly font that Lissy had started fiddling with. "The infographic. The carcass at least."

"Does it have to be pink?" Nate asked, looking as pained as if she'd handed him a set of knitting needles and asked him to make her a pair of bootees.

"Pink's romantic. And hot-pink's…well, *hot*."

Nate muttered something that sounded along the lines of, *This can't possibly be worth it.*

"I've got some great stuff to work with so far: one in five singles have tried online dating. Less than one percent believes a movie is a good idea for a first date. More than half of women think dinner is a good first date, and that the guy should pay—"

"You refused to let me pay."

"I'm not most women."

"So you keep reminding me."

"Here." She dug through the pile on her left, found the legal pad dedicated to that job, and threw it to him.

He moved the chair closer. Close enough that when she next swung back her knee brushed his. Thick wool rasped against old denim and the friction shot through her as if she'd been hit with a cattle prod.

His eyes widened as he flipped page after page of the questions she'd come up with in her research. Some of them she'd already put into a survey she'd added to the Dating By Numbers website, and given to a handful of online magazines—men's and women's. Others were just of interest to her.

She glanced down at the pages, reading words such as *sex, love, lies, oral, psycho killer, back-up plan.* She slowly slid a pen towards Nate. "It's the intimate details that lift a piece from dry statistical analysis to something that resonates with people. So if you have anything you'd like to add—thoughts, experiences, anything—feel free. Start simple. Like, are you a leg man?"

Nate's face began to turn green.

"Eyes, then? Hair? Little toes? If you picked me, clearly it's not about chest inches. Or is it something more intangible? Something chemical?"

His eyes shot back to hers at that, so blue, so quick, so effortlessly seductive, and she could have kicked herself for getting cocky.

He put the notepad back onto her desk, holding her gaze the whole time. "You really want to know what I like?"

She did. She really did. "Hit me."

"I like drinks—casual, no promises. I like parties—more people to talk to if talking to *her* is like pulling teeth. I like night time—it has a built-in end point."

"Wow. That all sounds so…hopeless."

"You asked," he said, grabbing a box of paperclips and shaking it by his ear as he leant back, his knees pressing deeper under her desk, crowding her, leaving her nowhere to move.

"Yeah," she said, tucking herself into a tighter ball on her chair, "I did." Then a thought. "Okay, then, what are you hoping for when you meet a woman? And I don't mean the 'built-in-end-point.' I mean *ultimately*."

His eyes narrowed and his jaw clenched. So many walls, she thought, wondering how he managed to connect beyond superficially with any member of the human race. The guy needed more than ruffling. He needed disentangling.

"Is this going to end up in your piece?"

She thought about it, and then shook her head. "*I* want to know."

"Why?"

She threw out her hands, her feet collapsing to the ground so that her knees bumped against his. "Because it's the human condition, Nate. Biological imperative. Haven't you ever had the urge to clobber some woman over the head and brand her as yours?"

Seeing the darkness in his eyes, she was pretty sure he was allowing himself a moment to imagine how his life might be better off if he clobbered *her* over the head.

He leant forward and put the paperclips back on the desk, then rested his elbows on his knees, his gaze settling at some point in the middle distance. He said, "This isn't for the piece. This is just for you."

She nodded. Swallowed. Gripped her mouse for support.

"After my father died I spent six long years of my life looking after the whims and needs of four very emotional, very demanding, very much loved women—and it near wiped me out. I've done my time on that score. I have no desire to 'settle down.' To marry. To 'make a life with someone.' Whatever you want to call it. I like women. Adore many. Love a handful. But I like my independence more. Ultimately I will protect it with my dying breath. How's that?"

"Thank you," she said, even as his words felt like little needles all over her skin.

"Your turn. Why do you care so much about what I want?" he asked, his long fingers tapping a soft beat on the table, his blue eyes roving over her face.

"That's not how this works."

"Says who?"

"Me."

"You think you're the boss in this scenario?"

"I'm the boss in *every* scenario."

His grin showed teeth, straight and many, and that rare and delightful dimple. "Well, sweetheart, in my world so am I. So what are we going to do about it?"

She had to swallow before she could get a word out. "I think you're a good guy, Nate. But when it comes to relationships you're screwed in the head. I think I can help."

"I'm beyond help. Do you want to know what I *need?*"

Saskia hoped he had no clue about the button he'd just pushed. That she was sitting there humming with the desperate need to know what he needed. What any man needed. She'd been searching for that answer her whole damn life, without success, and Nate was about to hand her the key.

She nodded, even while the look in his eyes told her she was agreeing to way more than she could ever have bargained for.

"I took the day off today."

She found herself oddly disappointed. "Are you okay?"

"I'm fine," he said with a low rumble of laughter. "I didn't go to work. That's the first weekday I've had off work in seven years. I looked it up. That's what I spent an hour of my first day off in seven years doing—looking up how long it had been since the last time I'd played hooky."

"So why did you play hooky?"

"You. Badgering me about relaxing more."

She got two raised eyebrows with that, which she could only meet with blank shock.

"And partly because I've known for a long time if I don't ease back I'm going to burn out. So I thought about going fishing, even drove down to the pier at Sorrento with grand ideas of dropping a line for squid. Turns out I'm a total wimp—it was just too damn cold so I turned around and came home. And of all the things I could have done with my day I came here. To see you. Do this."

He reached out and ran a hand down her hair. A curl gripped his finger before he gave it a gentle tug.

"And this."

His hand moved to her neck. His eyes followed as his thumb ran down her throat.

"And this."

His hand roved over her shoulder, sliding her oversized sweater right along with it till her shoulder was bare. He swept his thumb over her collarbone and she shivered, pleasure pulsing through her.

With that he grabbed the arms of her chair and tugged till it was between his thighs. Anticipation raged inside her. It had been building since that night at the bar, and she'd used up the last of her resistance.

"Kiss me," he insisted.

She didn't need to be asked twice. She was in his lap, her hands in his hair, her mouth on his, before he took his next breath.

No testing this time. No figuring one another out. They just opened to one another—mouths, lips, teeth, tongues, breath intertwining as sexual tension wrapped about them like a tight coil.

Then, with a final slow swipe of his tongue along hers, Nate pulled back, his forehead leaning on hers. Their stilted breaths matched, mingled.

"Are we done here?" he asked, his voice like an echo deep inside a cavern.

"In what capacity?" she asked.

"I don't want to talk about other women."

"I don't want to hear it."

"Good."

Then, with a speed that defied the guy's impressive size, Nate slid an arm beneath her and lifted her into his arms. With a wholly unladylike *whoop* Saskia flailed her legs madly and she gripped his neck so hard she was sure she'd leave a mark.

His eyes slid to hers, dark, devilish, dangerous. "I'd be very happy to sweep everything off that desk of yours right about now."

"No!" The computers were leased, and she'd never get her notes back into order! "My room!" she said, pointing the way.

Nate hitched her as if she weighed next to nothing. "No, wait, it's being painted." She tugged at the near-dry curl curving against her cheek.

"Sasssskia…" he growled.

"What?"

The glint in his eye said everything.

"Screw it," she said, and wriggled out of his strong arms.

She pressed him right to the wall in the hall, tugged at his sweater, her mouth going dry at the flash of sinew and muscle, the smattering of golden hair on his chest, the darker trail curling about his navel before disappearing down the front of his jeans, and the eye-popping bulge a few inches lower.

She practically tore his T over his head, her hands at his chest, running eagerly down the bumps and planes. Her mouth followed, revelling in his taste, his insane heat, the thunder of his heart.

When she reached Nate's belt line he had other ideas.

He spun her about, pressing her against the wall, making a newly hung picture down the hall bounce precariously. Nate braced his hand against the wall by her head, wrapped the other around her back. The press of his hard body left her in no doubt as to how much he wanted this. Wanted *her*.

Desire rose inside her, scraping at her insides.

She slid a hand behind his neck, lifted onto her toes and kissed him for all she was worth.

"Why do you always taste so amazing?" he groaned against her neck.

"Goats' milk soap," she breathed. "It's my one descent into unadulterated decadence. Have to drive to the Dandenongs to buy it. Costs a mint."

This was met with silence.

"It's lush. You should try it."

"Don't worry. I am." With that his tongue lapped the rise of her collarbone, sending shivers so hard and fast through her body her knees gave way.

Luckily Nate was there to slide his knee between hers, pinning her to the wall.

"I got you," he said, and proceeded to show her just how by lifting both arms above her head and dragging her sweater off in one swift move, leaving her in a pink bikini top and a wave of goosebumps which Nate proceeded to kiss until each and every one melted away.

"Your grand renovation include a pool?" he said, his thumbs running along the underside of her bikini top.

"Laundry day," she said, her voice croaky as a whole new wave of goosebumps followed his touch. This time he let them be, till she squirmed at the pleasure and the pain.

His hands learnt her curves, what little there was of them, but the hitch in his breath, the reverence of his touch made her feel like a pin-up. The pulse of desire between her legs now so insistent it was a wonder he couldn't hear it.

And then his head dipped to kiss the swell of her breasts. When his teeth grazed her nipple through her bikini top, and then he sucked it into his mouth, leaving the fabric moist in the fiery air, her hands moved to his head, desperate to stop the ache, desperate for more.

Then he was down on his knees, kissing each of her ribs, dipping his tongue into her navel, rolling her tights down her legs, scraping his teeth over a hipbone, hitting every sweet spot and a few more she hadn't even known she had.

As he came back up his hands slid over the backs of her legs, behind her trembling knees, caressing her weakening thighs, grabbing her ass and pressing her against him—which was when she came to from the drenching red haze of desire enough to realise he was naked too. And ready. So ready.

She ran a hand over his perfect backside, glorying in the heat of him, the hardness, the pure and utter masculinity. She wondered how she'd ever thought him cool, untouchable. This was as real as it got.

He lifted her knee to wrap it about his hip. The heft of him was nudging at her core. She bucked at the sensation, her body pressing back, moving with him of its own accord, desperate to bring all this swirling need to completion.

She jumped into his arms, trusting him not to let her fall.

His eyes found hers—so hot, so dark, so intense—as if awaiting her final *yes*. She kissed him—open-mouthed acquiescence.

With his hands on her backside and a groan at her mouth, he pressed into her achingly gently, with more restraint than she could have managed. When she sighed, and pressed back, he finally drove into her, deep, full, a millimetre from too much. Then deeper again, till she had to pull away from his kiss to catch even the tiniest breath.

She closed her eyes, blind to all but the thick, rich, heady sensation pummelling her every which-way. It was too much. It was impossible. It was everything. And all too soon every skerrick of feeling contracted to a single point where her whole world stilled, throbbed, pressed in on her like the most beautiful pressure she never wanted to end.

But end it did—in a splintering of sensation that rent a shout of pleasure from her so loud her own ears rang.

Nate took her scream in his mouth, muffling the sound with a kiss so lush, so tender, she felt lost. As if she'd fallen anyway. Was falling still—even as he held her tight and pinned her to the wall with his final thrusts before his release came.

Trembling, spent, her muscles quivering in afterglow—or aftershock—she held on tight, her hands gripping his slick shoulders, her legs clamped to his hard hips.

He let her down slowly, easing out of her with infinite care—not as if they'd just had blinding hot sex against the wall, but as if she was something soft and precious. Even as her feet found purchase she was shaking so hard there was no way she'd be able to stand upright.

"I got you," he said again, hands on her hips, forehead resting against hers, keeping her steady.

She could feel the deep staccato beating of his heart, and was overwhelmed to find it as erratic as her own.

Real, she thought. He felt so real. And for a silly little moment she wished it *was* all real. Him, this, her feelings. Everything.

Which snapped her smartly back to real life. To the fact that she wanted it all and he wanted nothing. To the fact that he was so fanatically independent he'd never budge enough to let someone take care of him. And that that was all she knew how to do.

"That was some renegotiation," she said, trying to snap the moment before it snapped her.

A beat bled by in which she wondered if she'd gone too far, made light of something too significant. Then his laughter rumbled through them both, deep and satisfying. "Wasn't it just?"

Nate trailed his hand from hip to arm and back again, and Saskia found it hard to hang on to reality at all.

"Why the hell did we not do this earlier?" he asked.

"From memory, we were being smart."

"Yeah? You're probably right." He bent down, gathered his gear. "Bathroom?"

She angled her head down the hall. "Second on the left."

He laid a kiss on her neck, followed by a quick swipe of his tongue, then walked that way, giving Saskia a superb view of beauty incarnate. A sexual dynamo. A frustrating, hardheaded, stubborn example of a man. A danger to the heart of any woman who crossed his charismatic path.

She was in so much trouble.

At the door he looked back. A grin spread across his face— a happy grin—leaving in its aftermath a clench in her belly that pierced the pleasure-induced numbness that held sway all through the rest of her. Then he shook his head once and disappeared.

Slapping a hand across her eyes, Saskia thanked her lucky stars the fire was still roaring as the night air cooled her damp skin. She was also thankful that she'd shaved her legs.

Crushing on Nate from afar was one thing. Sharing a few kisses was flirting with danger. But what had just happened—that inferno of desire, that wanton drive to take and be taken... It was still too soon. Her body was still humming from the effects, all of her too damn raw, to decipher what that was.

The old cuckoo clock in her lounge room cuckooed—seven o'clock.

Lissy!

She reached for her phone to turn Lissy around before she arrived with Indian, then realised she was butt-naked and her phone was nowhere to be found. In a flash of inspiration, she grabbed her bikini top from the floor, quickly opened the front door and hung it from the handle outside and slammed the door shut.

It was no tie on the door, but it would have to do!

When Saskia turned back, Ernest—tail wagging, eyes bright—met her nose to nose.

"Hey buddy," she said. "Did you catch any of that?"

Ernest gave her nose a gentle lick of support.

"I know, the guy brought Oreos. This too shall pass, but we can have some fun till then, right?"

Ernest thumped his tail on the floor before sliding across the floorboards to his possie in the lounge. One thump was for yes, right?

She heard the shower being turned on. Her head kicked in that direction. That shower was touchy. Only right she should show her visitor how it worked.

CHAPTER SEVEN

FIRST THING MONDAY morning Saskia sat in the foyer at Dating By Numbers, humming to herself. Her eyes roved happily over the golden-framed artwork, the fresh flowers on every surface, the discreetly frosted glass walls, the thick white carpet that must be a bitch to keep clean.

With many online businesses run from a home offices these days, instead the dating site took up the top floor of a beautiful old building in elegant Kew. It seemed there was a lot of money to be made in facilitating the search for true love. And in random hook-ups, one night stands, invites to friends of friends' weddings...

"Saskia? Marlee Kent," said a tall, elegant woman with a slick dark bob. She could have been aged anywhere from early forties to late fifties.

Saskia pulled herself from the overly soft couch and shook the woman's hand, before following her through padded velvet doors into a discreetly elegant office beyond, where on a tidy desk sparkled two big glass bowls—one filled with Baci chocolate kisses, the other with condoms.

"So you joined the site?" Marlee asked as they sat, her long red nails wrapped around the handle of an old-fashioned china coffeepot as she poured without asking how Saskia liked it.

Saskia reached into her bag for her yellow legal pad. "I did. A few weeks back."

"And what did you think?"

"It's very thorough. As a researcher, I like thorough."

Marlee's smile didn't reach her eyes. "And you've found someone?"

"Excuse me?" Saskia said, wondering if it was written all over her face that she'd been on the receiving end of some very hot and thorough loving only a couple of hours before, when Nate had turned up at her door before work for a breakfast special.

"You mentioned a case study in your email?"

"Oh. Yes. Well, studying him, getting the man's perspective, has been most helpful."

"I see." Marlee clearly saw plenty, as that time the smile did reach her eyes. "Then my job here is done."

"No," Saskia said, her cheeks threatening to ripen like a tomato. "It's not like that. We're not…romantically involved." Financially, sexually, mutually helpingly, at times frustratingly, but *not* romantically.

After he'd left that first night she'd found the dossier. Her heart had fluttered as she'd opened it, her stomach tumbling as she'd giddily imagined what he'd revealed to her only to find a few random titbits such as his favourite footy players, how he liked his coffee, the phone number of the best dry cleaner in East Melbourne. She'd thought he'd turned a corner. Instead he'd given a lollipop to quieten a noisy toddler.

And while Nate might be charming, hot as the sun and could make her melt with a whisper of breath, the touch of his lips, the slide of a hand, even *after* he'd given her the most exquisite sex of her life, she didn't feel any closer to breaking down that door.

"So, honey," said Marlee, gently breaking into her reverie, "what do you need from me?"

"Well, okay," Saskia said, pulling herself together. "I have the preliminaries down. Stats nearly done. The who, how old, how many—the dry substance. But it always helps to have a hook. A cheeky bite to get people talking over the water cooler. I had a crazy idea for a formula—"

She shook her head. It wasn't going to happen. Not right now anyway. Maybe one day. Maybe she'd have to rely on her own experience to nail that one.

"Now I'm thinking about the lies people tell in the search for The One."

"Such as?"

"Age, weight, interests, experiences. From what I saw, people lie about everything. But how will they ever be able to find someone who loves them just the way they are if they're not being honest about who they are?"

"You're a romantic."

"Aren't you?"

Marlee's laughter twinkled with just the right quality. Saskia shot her eyes to the glass bowls, afraid they might shatter.

"We discourage it, of course, in our welcome pack—lying about oneself, not romance—but you can't stop people from morphing the truth. It's human nature. I blow-dry my hair, put on make-up, wear high heels. I've laughed at jokes told by men who simply weren't that funny. We create an outer identity to hide our innate vulnerability. But even deeper, it springs from the most primal desire we harbour—to land the alpha male."

Saskia looked down at her notes, her pen hovering, but she wasn't sure where to start. Marlee's claim made scientific sense, and yet *she'd* never tried to land an alpha male. The men she dated were barely even betas.

Funny, she'd picked on Nate for fighting against the human condition, the biological imperative, and it seemed she was doing the same. Huh! At least now she'd gone alpha, she could see the appeal.

Putting Nate out of her mind as best she could, she said, "So you think it's natural to lie? Even when looking for love?"

Marlee steepled her fingers beneath her chin as she looked

Saskia dead in the eye, her heavily made up eyes hypnotic. "Are *you* looking for love, Saskia?"

Saskia swallowed. "Oh, sure. Of course. Well, not right now. There have been…men. And it hasn't worked. For myriad reasons." *Like grand theft.* "But I'm sure I'd welcome it if it came calling. Wouldn't we all?"

Marlee shrugged—a spiky lift of her sharp shoulders. "Everyone's different. Some people want it so badly you can see the desperation pouring off them in waves. Others want it less than root canal. You, on the other hand, confuse me, Ms Bloom. You have a neat little figure, just-rolled-out-of-bed hair, with a little more make-up your eyes could be stunning, and yet with all that potential you dress like you've walked off the set of *Oliver.* I'm a scholar of human body language, and you don't give off the usual signs at all."

While Saskia reeled under this blatant and not altogether flattering character assessment, Marlee brought her coffee to her red lips, her dark bob swinging precisely against her cheek as she took a sip. "What does love look like to you, Saskia Bloom?"

Saskia's mouth popped open before slamming closed. Because the truth was she had no idea.

"Perhaps the thing isn't lying about who you are, but misrepresenting your true desires—whatever they are."

Saskia's brain sifted through all this new information as if it was creating a fresh Rolodex.

"So, does your young man know how you feel about him?"

"My young *who?*" Saskia said, shoving her legal pad back in her bag and practically shoving her head in with it to hide the rush of blood to her cheeks.

"Darling, this is my field, and I make a fine living at it. Lie to me, lie to him—I don't care. Just don't be silly enough to lie to yourself."

Saskia closed her eyes shut tight, stopped fiddling and with

a sharp outshot of breath that flicked a curl skyward she looked
at Marlee and asked, "How?"

"Take a breath. Still your mind. Forget yourself. Follow
your heart."

"Now *you* sound like the romantic."

"Do I?"

Saskia left not long after, her head spinning with everything
Marlee Kent had given her. There were nuggets of gold for the
infographic, quotes galore she and Lissy could weave into the
piece. But as for the rest?

She knew she wanted to love and be loved. Growing up
near invisible to the only family she'd ever had, she'd known
that since before she even knew what the want deep in her
belly meant.

As for what love *looked* like? On that score she'd done what
she'd always done and used her head. She'd played the numbers, and shortened the odds by choosing men according to
how her skill set would complement theirs. She was energetic,
organised, liked being in charge and was quietly terrified that
she was unlovable. And therefore had gravitated to a string of
losers who'd…proven her theory over and over again.

Forget yourself, Marlee had said. *Follow your heart.*

Once at her car, Saskia stuck her key in the driver's-side
door—the remote locking hadn't worked since Stu had hit the
thing with the moving truck—then bumped the crumpled panel
with her hip to pop the door open.

Take a breath. Still your mind.

She'd tried that after Stu had left, she honestly had. Even
going so far as to attend a couple of Lissy's power-yoga classes,
which had sounded like a contradiction in terms and turned
out to be exactly that.

But she'd been burned so badly she'd not have found love
if it had jumped up in front of her with a flashing sign telling
her what it was.

At least she was back on her feet financially and would soon be able to cut back on her overwhelming workload. She'd have time to breathe, time to date again. And maybe this time she'd give herself half a chance; with a little less fear, a little more forethought, a little more faith.

After the wedding.

After Nate.

She stuck the key in the ignition and then let her hand drop.

Marlee had told her not to lie to herself, and the God's honest truth was that with the swarm of foreboding the woman had whipped up inside of her, *all* she wanted to do was go to Nate.

It was the strangest feeling. In fact it close to feeling a heck of a lot like *need*. Her hand shook a little as she dialled his mobile number. Shaking her hair from her ear, she waited for him to pick up.

"Saskia," he said.

And even while she told herself it was mental, financial, sexual, mutually helpful, at times frustrating, his voice sent happy goosebumps all over her skin. "Can I come over tonight?"

When silence ensued she clamped her eyes shut tight and said, "Ever since you described your place I've imagined a deer head on the wall above your bed. I can't sleep for not knowing if I'm right."

"Well," he said finally, "I'd hate to be the reason you can't sleep. How's eight?"

"Eight's great."

"Bring your PJs. For helping with the sleeping."

"One problem with that."

"Hmm?"

"I never wear any. No word of a lie."

"Texas," Saskia said, her voice far away, drowsily running her finger around the edges of the birthmark on Nate's naked thigh. "I honestly see Texas."

"It's roundish," he murmured, lifting his heavy head a half an inch off the padded edge of his big deep tub before letting it drop. His fingers never stopped trailing lazily up and down her feet, which were propped on his shoulder.

Saskia slipped an inch lower, revelling in the hot water, the decadent bubbles, the dreamy sound of Nat King Cole playing through Nate's fancy system, too deep in afterglow to do much more than blink fuzzily at the fake—as it turned out—rhinoceros head suspended on the stark grey wall over Nate's shoulder.

"Unless you're a contortionist," she said, "or handy with a mirror, you'd never know."

"I've been told. By women of good authority."

"How's that? Did your sisters pin you down and measure it out?"

"Never happened," he rumbled in warning. "I might be outnumbered, but I'm smart. And crafty. And strong."

Before she even felt him move he tugged, nearly dunking her under the wash of spicy-scented bubbles. She came up spluttering as he pulled her feet apart and drew her towards him till there was nothing to do but straddle his thighs and grab his big shoulders.

"Evidently," she said, settling. The hairs of his legs rasped against all too sensitive skin.

She wiped the bubbles from her hair, and twisted the length over her shoulder.

Nate's eyes followed the movement, changing to a darker shade of heaven as he watched the trail of water wavering down her collarbone, over the rise of her breasts where bubbles slid south. His knees lifted, pressing her forward, nudging her centre against the thickness of his.

"What was it like?" she asked. "Growing up with sisters."

As soon as the words came out of her mouth she stilled, waiting for him to shut down. For the worshipping touch of his eyes to cloud over.

"Loud," he said, surprising her.

Saskia breathed out.

"I'm not sure if it's a female thing, or a Mackenzie female thing, but no matter how I laid down the law they could never keep their hands off my stuff."

Saskia didn't have any sisters to compare them to, but she thought of Lissy, of the pieces of Lissy's clothing hanging in her closet, the books and DVDs of hers lost in the depths of Lissy's apartment. "Female thing, I think. Bonding, perhaps? Nesting, maybe?"

"What was it like growing up with no sisters?"

"Quiet."

He cocked a half smile.

"Especially when my father would have preferred to spend a beautiful spring day in the university library rather than playing in a park."

"And what was she like? Your mother?"

"Dad didn't talk about her much. Only when he saw her in me. When I was acting 'too colourful,' as he put it."

"He never married again?"

"He never married at all. From the bits and pieces I managed to gather I came to think of my mum as a free spirit—his one brief shining moment and his cautionary tale." She'd seen them try though—students, fellow scholars, even a Dean or two, but her clever, handsome, distant father had remained impassive. Married to his work, they'd all sigh, only Saskia had seen the rare flashes of pain that would pass over his eyes when he looked at her, as if he was seeing her mother…the one who ruined him for all others. And knowing it, she'd tried harder to make it all better.

"I at least had my dad till I was into my teens. Long enough to identify what it meant to be a man," he said, surprising her again.

Saskia swallowed at his words. At the thought of a boy of fifteen having to take on that mantle. When his eyes found hers, she said, "It was what it was. Maybe easier because I never knew any different."

"Maybe. Now, promise me…"

Anything. "Mmm?"

"Not a single thing we've done together had better end up in that damnable pink thing of yours."

"Hmm…" His eyes connected with hers, a smile curling at the corner of his sensuous mouth.

Then his hands left her hips to dig into the flesh at her waist. Saskia's eyes fluttered shut, her mouth tipping open as he rocked her forward, creating the most gorgeous pressure inside her.

But her head was filled with so many more questions. About his childhood, his family, his relationships, his choices. How they'd all intertwined to make him who he was. To keep him from getting close to someone special. Because whether it was the water, the lethargy, the bubbles, the fact that they hadn't stopped touching one another for even half a second, *something* had relaxed him, given him ease.

When his hand lifted to run down her torso, from collarbone to belly, the questions fled. When he took her hips, his thumbs sweeping her inner thighs, she struggled to remember her own name.

He lifted to kiss her neck, nip at her shoulder, to draw her wet nipple into his mouth. His hand moved between them, sliding along her seam with gorgeous restraint. Another finger followed, with less restraint, and while a minute before she would have considered herself spent, from one heartbeat to the next she felt drenched with desire. Her eyes were unseeing, her breath a mere instinct. She wrapped her arms around his head, pressed against him, took his fingers inside as he held her tight, and rode the arc of exquisite need.

There was that word again.

"Nate?" she whispered.

"Shhh…" he said, before taking her mouth with his, his hot, slick lips feeding her the most devastating kisses of her life.

And any disquiet dissolved into a haze as he pulled back and locked his gaze to hers, the stunning blue so dark with desire emotion rose thick and fast within her, expanding till it filled her all the way to her throat. There it stopped, as pleasure and pressure built inside her, and from there it was released, and the roar of his name echoed off the walls as she fell apart.

Truly spent, Saskia collapsed into Nate's arms. He held her there, a hand tracing her spine, the other twisting her hair as wave after beautiful wave of aftershock trembled through her.

Feeling the pound of Nate's heart against her own, Saskia took a breath, stilled her mind, forgot herself and heard her own heart.

This, it said.

And she knew exactly what it meant.

Nate Mackenzie might not talk about himself as much as she wished, but when she was with him he was more present than any man she'd ever known.

He was the first man who'd ever been with her not because he needed to be but because he *wanted* to be. And that made more of a difference than she'd ever imagined.

But not Nate, she told her heart. *Not him.*

It said nothing back. It seemed her heart had exhausted its wisdom for the moment.

"We ever going to actually make it to a bed, do you think?" she said, her voice thick.

"One of these days."

She felt Nate's smile against her shoulder. And then his teeth scraped over her rose tattoo before he replaced them with a gentle kiss. She didn't need to count to know exactly how many days they had left together. It was permanently imprinted on her brain, like the ticking of a time bomb.

"In fact…" said Nate, and he dragged himself upright, bubbles and water slewing over his glorious golden skin, till he stood before her, a supreme example of manhood in every which way.

Then he pulled her to her feet, threw her over his shoulder, and padded out of the ridiculously large *en suite* bathroom, into his bedroom which, with its elegant striped wallpaper, leather-backed bed and dark wood trim, looked as if it had come straight out of the set of *Mad Men*.

"Wow!" she said, her hands on his hips. "Testosterone central."

"The faux rhino wasn't evidence enough? Told you—the designer went mad."

He gave her bottom a kiss before throwing her on the bed. She bounced and settled, still covered in bubbles, and watched as he found a condom, slid it into place, his eyes roving over her wet, naked form as if he couldn't decide where to start...

Later, Saskia lay sated beneath luxurious sheets. Nate's arm was slung heavily across her hip, hooked so his hand settled between her breasts, and the tips of his long fingers were close enough to kiss.

In that soft place between awake and asleep, with the hot, hard length of him nestled in behind her, the last thing that entered her mind before consciousness finally eluded her, was:

This.

Saskia woke to the sound of a phone ringing. One eyelid at half-mast, she reached out for it—only to knock over a big rectangular lamp with an elephant built into the base, and an Art Deco clock from a low mahogany bedside table.

Nate's bedside table.

Her eyes popped open like a Pop-Tart in a toaster. She'd slept over? She'd slept *over*. Oh, God! She'd only meant to drift off for a few minutes, regain some strength, then kiss him to distraction before heading off into the night as if what they were playing at was nothing but fun and games.

Not...not what her heart had hinted at the night before. The same heart that now gave her an unfamiliar little squeeze hello. She shut the thing down and glanced over the side of the bed at the clock on the floor to see it was some time after ten, meaning Nate would be long gone.

He could have woken her, though, sent her on her way before he left. She couldn't help but feel a little chuffed that he'd trusted her enough to leave her be. Unless he had really good security.

Her phone rang again, and she kicked at the charcoal-grey bedding hooked around her legs, then rushed naked to the chunky leather *chaise* in the corner of the huge room. Rummaging in her massive bag, she found her phone. Withheld number. Probably a client.

Sitting, naked, with a *whump* on the edge of the couch she answered, "SassyStats. Saskia Bloom speaking."

"Hi, Saskia!" twin voices shouted down the phone.

No. It couldn't be.

"It's Hope," said one.

Then, "And Faith. We nicked your number from Nate's phone the day you came over. Anyhoo, we have a free morning and thought how nice it would be to get to know you better—considering."

Considering what? That she was sitting on their brother's *chaise* naked? She grabbed a deep red afghan and covered herself to her neck.

"We thought coffee at Chadstone?" said one.

The other added, "Then shopping. Hope's a stylist, so she'll find you the perfect thing."

"For…?"

"The wedding! Two birds with one stone."

Saskia wondered momentarily what these two birds would do with a stone if they knew her relationship with their beloved brother was all a lie.

"Please say you'll come," Hope said hopefully.

Saskia nibbled at her bottom lip.

Saying no would seem plain rude, which wouldn't help Nate's cause. And she'd not actually considered what she'd wear to the wedding. Clothes weren't really her thing, and considering her finances it had been months since she'd been able to afford even to update her undies.

And then it hit her—she knew how much Nate hated talking about himself, so using him as her infographic/love formula test bunny had been harder than getting blood from a stone. But he'd never expressly asked that she not talk to his family.

Three birds with one stone...

"I do need a dress," she said, and Faith near deafened her with excitement as she barked orders down the phone as to when and where they'd meet.

Only after she'd hung up the phone and was taking advantage of Nate's enormous dual-headed shower—keeping her back to the fake rhinoceros head which seemed to watch her no matter where she was in the room—did she wonder if she should have checked with Nate first.

But, no matter how it looked, he wasn't her boyfriend. So as long as she kept within the bounds of their agreement he didn't get a say. Besides, he would have said, *No way in hell.*

She wasn't as convinced that she'd made the right decision an hour later as Faith and Hope curled their grips into the crooks of her elbows and dragged her all over Chadstone.

"You even smell like him, you know," said Faith, as they hit the top of the escalator and headed towards designer row.

Saskia sniffed her shoulder, and realised she did. "Must be his shower gel," she said, a moment before realising what she'd just given away. "Too much information."

"No. You have no idea how happy it makes me." Hope gave her a happy bump with her hip. "We were all beginning to think he was actually *serious* in his efforts not to settle down. And then you came along and we all let out a long, thankful breath."

"Oh. Right." Saskia bit her lip to stop herself saying anything more. Even while she knew Nate would be thrilled to the tips of his designer socks that his sisters were so far off the scent, she'd never counted on the fact that they'd see her as anything other than the last in a long line of future exes. That they'd care.

A little twinge of guilt took up residence in her belly.

Saskia was down to her bra and undies in a change room when Faith's voice sing-songed from the other side of the curtain. "Think of the babies you two would make. Sweet, serious little things that'd charm a lolly out of a candy machine."

Saskia poked her head around the edge of the huge velvet curtain as the guilt began to churn. "Faith, I—" *God, how to put this?* "Nate and I are having a really good time together, but *babies* are…not on the agenda. Yet. For a good long while. If at all. Okay?"

"We *know,*" said Faith, holding the netting of a fascinator over her eyes as she pulled kissy faces at a nearby mirror.

The way she said it made the guilt churning in Saskia's stomach turn to lumps.

"You know *what,* exactly?" Saskia called, grabbing at the heavy velvet curtain which kept slipping out of her grip.

"About the pre-engagement," said Hope, who now came at her from nowhere with a filmy, frilly red dress that looked like something out of a gangster movie.

Saskia held out a finger to take the hanger. "I'm sorry— the pre-what?"

Hope angled her head behind Saskia and she glanced back to see that her cotton-covered backside was in full view of the store in the mirror at her back. She let the curtain swing closed and looked at herself, cheeks pink, hair a tumble, the red dress clutched to her front like a great figurative scarlet letter.

CHAPTER EIGHT

"YOU TOLD YOUR family we are *pre*-engaged?"

Nate looked up from the conference table, where he and Gabe were knocking back double espressos and doughnuts as they strategised the next step in landing a new account, to find Saskia barrelling down on him, her face a mask of fury.

Too many things hit him at once.

First, Saskia was looking about as damn cute as any woman had the right to look, even in an odd get-up of tight army pants, cropped leather jacket, mottled scarf and huge floppy beanie.

Next, Saskia's brow was furrowed, her sultry eyes wild, cheeks pink, lips a deep red—as close to how she looked when she fell apart in his arms as he'd ever seen her in daylight.

Lastly, Saskia had apparently been talking to his family.

"Pre-engaged?" Gabe repeated, when Nate said nothing at all. Then Gabe laughed, the deep sound echoing off the walls of glass enclosing the imposing room.

Saskia's fiery gaze shot to Gabe and she stuck a hand on her hip and nodded. "I know, right? What the hell is *pre*-engaged anyway? A man made that up, for sure. As a way to get out of ever actually being engaged."

"You got that right," Gabe said. "If you want a woman you get married. No in between."

"Thank you!"

"What kind of bling do you get for being pre-engaged?" Gabe asked, turning in his chair to direct that one to Nate, his dark eyes laughing their proverbial asses off. "Semi-precious at best."

Nate angled his head at Gabe then towards the door. *Out. Now.*

"Oh, no, no, no," Saskia said, waggling her finger at them both. "Of all the men in this room right now I like him best. So he can stay. Why not? He might know more about our 'burgeoning relationship' than I do."

Wheels in his head whirring back to life, Nate stood, planted his hands on the table with a thump, and said, "Enough, Saskia. Calm down. Sit."

"Excuse me?" she said, her eyes like twin flints.

He should have known better than to tell her to calm down, what with having three sisters, but this woman messed with his synapses. And *hell* if seeing her all riled didn't turn him on…

He eased back in his chair with a studied air of submission. "Have a doughnut."

Saskia blinked. Then her eyes cut to the tray of doughnuts on the table beside the mini-espresso machine. She licked her lips. Once. Enough for Nate to feel it in his groin. Then she shook her head so hard the curls below the edge of her beanie slapped her in the face.

Nate felt Gabe wince beside him.

"Sit," he said again, then after a breath softened it with, "Please? And we'll talk. Alone."

"Fine, fine."

Gabe dragged his bulk from the chair and ambled out—but not before planting a kiss atop Saskia's head. And for that Nate wanted to crack *him* over the head with the nearest chair.

Saskia took a deep breath through flaring nostrils before she sat. Once she did, she seemed to deflate, head in hands, toes just touching the floor, as if she was trying to make herself as small as possible.

Swearing beneath his breath, Nate unclenched his hands from his chair's armrests and rounded the table, took the seat beside hers. "Start at the beginning. How is it that you were talking to my family at all?"

She drew her hands down her face—eyes smudged, cheeks now devoid of colour, lips turned down at the corners. He actually wished the banshee was back.

"The twins rang this morning and invited me out shopping to find a dress to wear to the wedding."

His sisters. His deal. His fault. He took her hands in his. Compared with his hot fingers they were soft and cool and small. "So you got a dress?"

"I did," she said, delight flaring in her eyes, colour swarming back to her cheeks, her mouth turning up gently at the corners. *She's something,* he thought. *Like there's a light inside of her determined to shine no matter what.* And he bet she hadn't a clue.

She looked up at him then, and breathed in deep, even a little shakily. "Why do they think we're engaged, Nate?"

"Pre-engaged," he said, unhooking a stray curl from her eyelash. "I have a small idea. Jasmine rang this morning—asking about you, about how things were going."

He'd been standing in his bedroom doorway at the time, wondering whether or not to wake Saskia. She'd been curled up in his bed asleep, hands tucked under her chin, knees drawn to her chest, toes coiled around one another, her riot of hair splayed across his dark pillow, her soft lips parted, her face clear.

He shifted imperceptibly on his chair and said, "I might have told her something along the lines of 'they're going in the right direction.'"

Saskia breathed again—a little more shakily, a little deeper.

He continued, "Then one of them—Faith, probably—called and asked when the 'Save the Date' cards were on their way. I said I had no clue what she was talking about. She explained, I said she was a good couple of steps ahead of herself and—"

"She took a natural two steps back and landed on pre-engaged."

"So it seems. The others are persistent, but at least they are vaguely sensible. I'm not sure where I went wrong with her."

Saskia turned his hands over and gave them a little squeeze. She must have hit a nerve, because warmth shot through him with all the subtlety of a bolt of electricity.

"Nate, I like your family, and I'm not sure how I feel about lying to them any more. Fudging a few dates is one thing, but *engaged?*" She leaned into the huge bag on her shoulder and pulled out a folded piece of paper. A cheque. Rumpled at the edges as if she'd worried at it some. "If you could wait a couple of months before banking it…"

As realisation hit panic swelled inside him. He clapped his hand around hers. "No!"

"Nate," she said, her eyes beseeching.

"Do you want more money?" Her head rose so slowly he knew he'd said the wrong thing. "I take that back."

"I can't believe you just said that!"

He ran a hand up the back of his hair. "Me either. I'm sorry. It's just…this was meant to be simple."

"And it's not, is it?" she asked, looking him right in the eye.

Brave girl. Braver than he. He gave himself a mental shake and simply refused to go there.

"Our initial contract was fulfilled the moment you stepped over my mother's threshold."

"But—"

"I mean it. All I really wanted them to believe was that I was seeing someone. You made that happen. Every moment from that point on was above and beyond."

"So the wedding…?"

A moment hovered in front of him—a moment during which he could have thanked her for her efforts and sent her on her way.

A savvy businessman, to say the least, he knew when to

take such moments. Cut ties and move on. The world was a big place with a million new deals to be made. And yet in that moment, even while they were surrounded by glass walls, with people walking past, glancing in, no doubt wondering who the small brunette with her foot tucked up on a chair, looking unblinkingly into their boss's face might be, the world felt about two metres square.

He looked into Saskia's big nearly brown eyes and heard himself say, "Tell me about the dress."

"Red," she said, swallowing. "Floaty. Gonna knock your socks off."

"I'll be sure to wear two pairs."

Her breath was released on a big sigh. He did much the same, only he was far better at hiding it.

"Okay," she said, frowning a moment, before adding, "But your family—"

"It's not a lie, Saskia. Not any more. The pre-engagement is Faith being Faith. But as for the rest...? You might not have noticed, but we're sleeping together. And we're exclusive. That's about as close to a relationship as I've ever been."

He actually held his damn breath as he waited for her response. Those big eyes were searching for the loophole. Poor kid. She'd been screwed over so many times by men who'd just wanted something from her she couldn't see when someone was being honest. And he was. He wanted her as his wedding date, and he wanted her in his bed until that day. Exclusively.

When her answer came it was, "Wow! A more romantic proposal I never did hear."

At which he laughed. Laughed till his sides hurt.

Then came a smile so sweet and unexpected it near broke his heart. Thankfully the thing was unassailable, tough as old leather, or he might have begun to worry.

"Why do I get the feeling I should have fought harder to cut you off?"

"Low blood sugar," he said, sliding the platter of dough-nuts her way.

Rolling her eyes, she lifted her backside off the chair and took one, biting into it with relish. "You're trouble, Nate Mac-kenzie. I should have known it the minute I saw you walk into Mamma Rita's. Heck, maybe I did see it and just didn't care."

"You're no walk in the park either, Saskia Bloom."

At that, she grinned. "Maybe we should shock them all and just get married. You can keep the losers from my door and I'll keep infuriating matchmakers from yours."

She was joking—he knew she was joking—and yet for a brief shining moment the simplicity of it made a perverse kind of sense: her contentment, her warm body, the way she made him laugh.

Until memories of skimpy underwear hanging over the shower rail began to flick through his mind. And *Pride and Prejudice* marathons, and drips of red nail polish on the bath-room sink, and never being able to find a piece of chocolate in the house as once it crossed the threshold it became fair game. And the tears. So very much rich, thick, swinging emotion to navigate every single day.

If you want a woman you get married. To Gabe it was that simple. While Nate's skin began to itch as if he'd come out in hives.

He stood, took her hands, and drew her to her feet. "Get out of here, Ms Bloom, before I take you up on that."

She hitched her bag over her shoulder and gave him a wonky smile. "No wonder you're so good at what you do; for a second there I nearly believed you."

Together they walked to the glass door. She tried to tuck her hair behind her ears but it sprang back, a mass of wild curls. The lift of her arm raised her sweater, exposing a sliver of skin, the dip of her waist. And as her hand reached for the handle he touched her there. His hand at her hip his thumb found skin, and her light body melted into him as if it had been waiting to do just that.

He let her go, and without a backwards glance she opened the door and walked away.

"I just had a terrible thought."

Saskia grinned as Nate's voice rumbled down the phone line. Phone tucked under her chin, she grabbed a corner of vinyl from the kitchen floor and tugged. "Do tell?"

"It's just over a week away and I still haven't got a wedding present. Mae didn't do the normal thing and send invites weeks before the wedding with a registry card attached—"

"You know a lot about weddings, my friend."

"I'm beloved. I get a lot of invites."

Saskia gave up, shucked her gloves and plonked herself on a red vinyl chair in the corner of the kitchen. "Any reason you've included me in your terrible thought?"

"You're a woman."

"Why, thank you for noticing."

"Sweetheart, I think we can safely say I would not have kissed you by the cab that first night if I hadn't noticed that pretty quick-smart."

"And I thought that was just for credibility."

A pause, then, "You probably believe in fairies too."

Saskia laughed, then sighed, then curled up on the chair and gave herself over to the bliss.

After the pre-engagement blow-out they'd hit a kind of flirty, easy peace. That night she'd gone to Nate's to watch a movie and eat takeaway. After a half-hour they'd both decided they ought to be doing something else, and had spent the better part of the night doing just that.

He'd turned up at hers with Chinese and red wine the next night and they'd managed to eat about half before other more pressing matters had taken over.

When he'd refused to take her money back she couldn't

remember feeling more relief in her whole life. And it hadn't been about the debt. Not even a jot. It had meant she had another week and a bit with Nate in her bed. In her life. In her heart. She'd always thought herself a smart woman. Clearly she'd been mistaken.

"So, what does my womanhood have to do with your shopping dilemma?"

"Would you care to do the honours?"

"Not on your life." It occurred to her a split second later that in the past she would have said yes. Without hesitation. Saying no felt…good. Evolved. A blessed relief that she'd said it and her world hadn't ended.

"But—"

"You have three sisters, Nate. And a mother. Any one of whom would jump at the chance to help."

That shut him up. It was kind of nice to know she could still render the man speechless.

"Mae's your friend now as much as she is mine."

Saskia's mouth twisted at that. She'd been to Mae's hen night the night before and had the time of her life. A pub crawl through the Irish pubs of Melbourne had turned into something else entirely when Mae had taken it upon herself to stop every man they met and ask him about their internet dating experiences. It had given Saskia—who always had a yellow legal pad on hand—enough in-depth research from the male point of view to create three infographics.

It had been a blast, but it had also meant she'd not seen Nate at all.

"Okay. Then care to come shopping with me?"

Saskia looked down at her overalls, her sticky hair, her paint-splattered hands. "Sounds like a treat. But no. Can't. I'm tearing up my kitchen floor."

Another pause. "On your own?"

"Unlike you, I don't see the need to hire people when I'm perfectly capable of doing it myself."

"Would you even know how to ask for help?"

"Sure," she said with a shrug. "If I didn't think I could do it better myself."

"I've never met anyone like you, Saskia Bloom."

"Nice try. Get the gift yourself." She hung up, the sound of his laughter still humming through her.

A week, she thought, staring at the sun shining through the small collection of red glass bottles lined up on her kitchen window. A week more of Nate and then...*nothing*. That was pretty much what she felt like when she let herself hear the clock ticking in the back of her head. As if the place he had in her life would leave a hole too big to fill.

Because what would happen post-wedding? Not just with Nate but his friends? She liked Mae. Genuinely adored Gabe's fiancée, Paige. Would she see them again? *Should* she?

She knew Nate wouldn't try to stop her. But could she, knowing they ran in the same circles as Nate? Something gave her the feeling that going cold turkey would be for the best. A little something that tightened around her heart every time she thought about it.

As if he felt her impending gloom Ernest came padding in and she threw him the crust of her ham sandwich which she'd saved. He sniffed the air, smelled that it wasn't an Oreo and padded away, his claws slipping on the part of the floor which was now down to raw wood.

The blessed kitchen floor, she thought, dragging herself from the chair. Another reason she loved doing the work herself. Keeping busy had always meant not having time to think about all the things missing from her life.

No mum, a barely there dad, soon no Nate...

She donned her gloves, grabbed a hunk of vinyl and ripped for all she was worth.

Nate knocked on Saskia's front door.

He couldn't stand still, rolling his shoulders and shifting

from foot to foot. It was ridiculous; he couldn't remember being this unsure about dropping in unannounced on a woman since he was seventeen-years-old and all fired up to ask Lily von Krum's police commander father if he could take Lily to the Scotch College formal.

Women liked him. Always had. He couldn't remember a time when women hadn't stopped in the street to gush over his baby blues.

But Saskia was different in myriad tiny little ways he found himself struggling to pin down even while they hummed around him like a field of fireflies. She wasn't easy, but neither did she go out of her way to be hard. She was just…who she was. And the equanimity at the heart of her still gave him a kick.

A kick in the pants to yank himself out of his own rut and be more a part of the real world—which was why he was standing at her door.

He'd moved to knock again when a scrambling from inside stopped him. The door bumped, then swung open to reveal a mass of kinky curls atop Saskia's dark head, her knuckles white as she gripped her dog by the collar, his wiry body shaking with glee.

"Hey, buddy," Nate said, stepping in to help.

"Nate?" she said, looking up in surprise at the sound of his voice. Then, "Your suit!"

Which was when Nate realised he probably ought to have made a detour to change.

"Dime a dozen," he lied, not about to tell her it was his lucky suit. Not *date*-lucky—he rarely had a problem there. More like deal-of-the-century-lucky. Too late now. He gave the dog a rub. Crinkly doggie hair came off in droves.

"Ernest! Be gone!" she said, and like that the dog was off.

Nate stood, as did she. In overalls three sizes too large. Her feet were bare, bar the chipped paint on her nails, and her hair had been dragged off her face by a headband with a feather poking out of the top.

Her eyes slid down his torso with a thoroughness that sent a surge through his bloodstream. But when she blew a curl from her forehead with a quick stream of air from the side of her mouth it hit him hard, right in the solar plexus. She looked…like she always looked. Soft, vibrant, her wardrobe choice more than a little off centre. And yet there was no denying his certainty that she was one of the most gorgeous women he'd ever known.

He reached out and flicked the feather. She crossed her eyes at it before sliding it from her hair, her cheeks pinkening.

"Ernest found it outside," she said, playing with the fronds. "He gave it to me as a gift." She glanced over her shoulder. "I really can't shop, Nate. Not right now. I'm in the middle of something."

"I'm not here to ask you to shop," he said, moving past her since she hadn't asked him in. "I'm here to help."

Her hand still on the door handle, she blinked at him as if she didn't even know what the word meant.

"Help," he repeated, pulling off his jacket and tossing it onto a pale green cabinet in the entrance hall, noting it was new. As was the heavy round mirror above it. He rolled up his sleeves. "As in pull vinyl. Or lay tiles. Or re-roof the joint. Whatever you need." When she continued staring at him as if he was talking Swahili, he said, "Have you never had a man offer his services before?"

At that she shook her head. And he believed her. In that moment he wished she had a little black book—just so he could track down every man who'd ever hurt her, used her, abused her, taken all she had to offer without taking the time to let her know she was appreciated, that she was something special. What he wanted to do to them was possibly excessive, but then if a man didn't aim high, then what was the point of aiming at all.

"I don't need help," she said.

"I don't much care what you think you need, Miss Bloom, so you're going to have to put up with me."

"Aren't you meant to be at work?"

"I'm the boss. I can be wherever the hell I want to be."

"Yes, sir," she mumbled.

"That's more like it."

"Ha! Don't get used to it, buddy."

"Hmm, the day I do will probably be the day we're done."

She flinched as if he'd slapped her. Then schooled her face as if nothing was wrong. He wanted to slap himself.

He couldn't help himself. Since the blow-out in his conference room, when he'd had the perfect chance to end things amicably and hadn't, he'd been all over the shop. Wanting her with a ferocity he couldn't contain, while at the same time constantly reminding her, and himself, of their imminent demise.

He peeled her hand from the door handle and slammed the door. Then he led her past the newly painted hallway—where did the woman find the time?—into the kitchen, to find a disaster area.

Bits of vinyl torn up all over, bits still stuck, a few gouges out of the floor as if she'd taken to it with a mallet and a chisel.

He looked over his shoulder to find her frowning at the floor. "We seem to have met an impasse."

The magnitude of the job hit him. Along with the fact that she ran her own business, and that he'd been stealing every spare moment she had, while hampering her work by refusing to help her out by being her lab rabbit.

He'd thought *he* worked hard, but the woman didn't rest. And as he watched her frown at the floor, as if her entire self-worth was wrapped up in whether or not she could strip vinyl, it occurred to him why. The loser boyfriends, her distant father and getting things done were all she thought she was good for.

It put his own reasons for working his ass off to shame.

"It's a big job, Saskia. Maybe you should call a tiler—"

"I can take care of myself."

"I know you can," said Nate. "I get the feeling you've done just that your whole life."

Looking into those big bedroom eyes, over that soft pink mouth, twisting sideways as she tried to deny the undeniable, Nate said, "Today it's my turn."

It wasn't a question. It was a promise. And after only the slightest of hesitations Saskia nodded, her eyes melted and she let him.

With a tear in the front pocket and a stain that might or might not be dog food on his knee, the pants of his lucky suit were officially ruined. But the vinyl was gone—every last dot of the damn stuff—and, covered in the sweat of a job well done, Nate felt amazing.

He'd ditched his shirt an hour before. Saskia's overalls hung from her waist, leaving her in a tank top. Her hair was plastered to her neck and cheeks with sweat and her cheeks were smudged with dust.

When she realised they were done she brushed her hands together and let out a great sigh. She looked up at him and grinned.

"Happy?" he asked.

"Delirious! Thank you," she said, shaking her head as if she was amazed at herself for having let him help at all.

He ran a thumb over a smudge on her cheek. "Partners in grime."

She laughed again, the sound husky. Her big, dark, sooty-lashed eyes blinked up at him. Filled with more than thanks. Filled with so many things he'd barely pinned one down before it floated dreamily to the next. And even while he was smart enough to understand them, and hard enough not to want them, using a finger to tilt her chin he kissed her.

Her hands fluttered to his bare chest, the soft touch searing him. And like that they kissed—gentle, sweet, exploring kisses—for so long he lost track of time.

Her hands slid over his shoulders, deep into his hair, and she lifted onto her toes, taking the kiss deeper. He lifted her, desire pouring through him like a relentless waterfall, and pressed her back till she hit the bench. He tore her overalls down her legs, lifted her tank top, fell to his knees. He kissed her belly. Her salty taste hit the back of his throat and he groaned. Her fingers drove tracks through his hair as his teeth found her hipbone. His tongue her belly button. His mouth her centre.

With such sweet sensuality she melted in his arms, coming with a shudder he felt mirroring his own.

Then he lifted her into his arms, her slick skin sliding against his as he took her into her bedroom. He peeled off her damp clothes. Pressed her hair from her face. Wiped away the grime with her tank, leaving her clean and glowing. So fresh and beautiful he felt it pierce his heart.

"What will you do when you don't have me around to do that to you?" he asked, steeling himself against the sensation, against her. Brutal as it was, he wanted to know she'd miss him. Needed to know she'd feel it when he was gone.

Her eyes narrowed. Glinted. And then her hands began a slow trek down her naked sides, dipping into the dips, curving over the curves, driving him into near insanity.

"I can take care of myself," she said, her voice low and clear. "Been doing so my whole life."

Nate's smile came from deep within. "Today it's my turn."

This time there was no hesitation. Saskia lay back on the bed, her arms behind her head, her eyes cloudy with desire as she let him take her to oblivion and back.

Her eyes, those gorgeous brown depths, lit with passion and need and bone-deep tenderness, looked right into him as he buried himself inside her slick heat, and he came harder than he remembered coming his entire life.

* * *

Nate lay in Saskia's big soft bed, staring at the rainbows shifting across the pale pink ceiling—moonlight glinting off the chandelier of colourful plastic discs. Her smooth, lean leg was entwined around his, her breath was shifting the hairs on his chest, the soft heat at her centre pressed against his side.

She sighed and he tilted his head to look at her.

"What's up?" he asked, his voice barely a croak.

"I will miss this," she croaked back, her fingers playing with the hair on his chest.

"Don't blame you."

"Though I'm not sure why I ever thought you charming," she said with a laugh.

She snuggled closer. And he let her. He'd miss it too. For a while. Then he wouldn't. That was how it went. Though when he tried to imagine going about his days without her in them, his nights without her warm body melted against him, he didn't like what he saw.

For a split second he allowed himself to imagine an *after*. A few more dates, a few more DVD sessions, a few more drinks with friends, a few more nights like this. Then he stopped himself.

He might be selfish, but he hoped he wasn't a selfish bastard.

He knew this was getting harder for her. He knew her feelings for him weren't purely sexual. She just wasn't that good a liar. But, while he'd be happy with a little more contentment in his life, she wanted happily-ever-after. And that wasn't something he was willing to deliver.

Start as you intend to finish, he told himself. *Be honest, friendly, and most important be resolute.* It was past time to begin the great unwind.

"The charm thing," he said. "It's all an act."

She moved onto her elbows and looked into his face, her eyes fierce as she said, "Don't you believe it."

He took her hand and held it at his chest as he tried to find the words he needed. The words he knew she'd need, which somehow mattered more.

"After my father died," he began, his eyes on the ceiling again, "after the effort of the following few years, I was running on empty. If I was ever going to run a business without being attuned to every employee's emotional up-and-down I had to…stop caring. It worked. I did what I had to do to— charmed, led astray, hedged, profiteered—to carve a life for myself. The life I wanted. And I have that. And it's enough."

"You need to give yourself more credit."

"I think I'm awesome. How's that for credit?"

Her eyes narrowed and her mouth twisted to one side. Cutest woman he'd ever known, he thought. He stroked his thumb across the corner of her mouth and her eyes closed dreamily.

He let his hand drop, kicking himself for undoing any headway his little speech might have made. But he'd get there. He had no choice.

"Promise me something?" he said. "When this is all said and done…"

"Anything."

"You'll give *yourself* more credit."

"I can do that. Promise *me* something."

Anything. It hovered on the tip of his tongue, but he couldn't offer that. "Hit me."

"Stay ruffled."

Then she lifted a hand and ran it through his hair gently, fondly, with an intimacy he wasn't sure he'd felt since he was a kid.

"Unruffled, you're pretty cute. Ruffled, you're just plain irresistible."

She was ruffled, soft, pink-cheeked. Her hair mussed, her eyes hot and wanting. She was the definition of irresistible. This precocious creature, this spark in his day, the laughter in his thoughts, the wild cat in his bed, with her pushy little digs she was the incitement to spread his wings.

He lifted his hand to her cheek, waited till she looked him in the eye, and said, "Resist."

She breathed deep, her shoulders lifting, and said, "I'm trying."

And then, belying her words, she slid over him, her softness melting into him, turning him hard as a rock.

She lifted to her knees, holding her hair from her neck as she sank over him. Arching her back, she lifted, nudged again and again. The touch sent her head rocking back on her neck, her mouth open, her skin pink all over.

He gripped her hips, took control, stroking her even while he throbbed with pressure that beat to the point of pain.

"There," she said on a gasp. "Right there."

"Bossy."

Her eyes focused on his and her cheeks came over all rosy as her eyes dropped to his mouth. "You like it," she realised, letting him an inch inside before pulling away.

"Yeah," he said through gritted teeth, "I really do."

And with that she slid over him, all silken and gorgeous demand, and pleasure tore through him like liquid heat, twisting him inside out. She rocked, making his whole world spin, till it imploded where their two hot bodies met.

As exhaustion and completion dragged him to sleep Nate knew. Helping her pull up her kitchen floor clearly wasn't enough. He had to do more. Make her understand how grateful he was. Know that she meant something to him even as he told her goodbye.

CHAPTER NINE

NATE WASN'T SURE how long he sat on the edge of Saskia's soft bed early the next morning, watching her sleep, remembering how he'd held her in the night, her head beneath his chin, his hand on her hip. But at some point she'd curled into a little ball on the edge of the bed. He wondered if she always slept that way or if she'd been making room for him.

Figuring it was too early for philosophising, he padded down the hall and into the main bathroom to splash water on his face.

And there, amongst the stash of pens and paint samples on her bathroom bench, he saw a yellow legal pad. Even at a glance he recognised the Dating By Numbers study, the questions he'd managed to avoid answering. Though apparently at some point somebody had—many had notes against them in a different-coloured pen, some with something that looked a heck of a lot like the words *Pub Crawl* scrawled in the margin.

Intrigue and a healthy dose of jealousy—because some other man had given her what he wouldn't—made him read on to find questions about intimacy, love, attraction, fear and faith. The kinds of things he'd rather eat dog than talk about at length.

And yet seeing her happy, curly scrawl racing all over the page it seemed to him a small thing she'd wanted—a few simple truths in exchange for all he'd asked of her.

He gazed down the hall to where she slept.

She'd put herself out there with his family, his friends, risking exposure, putting up with his irascibility. The woman had

had her faith in people trodden on time and again, and yet her generosity was so hardwired she'd do the same thing all over again if he asked.

While *he'd* thrown a few bloodless titbits into the damn dossier as if they were some kind of gift. Because without thought, without care, he'd hardwired himself to *resist* anything remotely intimate.

He gripped the legal pad tighter in his hand as he was hit with a wave of disappointment. In himself. He *was* a selfish bastard. A wholly self-made one at that. Independence was one thing—grudging self-interest quite the other. That wasn't the kind of man he'd hoped to be one day—not even within spitting distance.

He found a pen, then, taking a deep breath, went through the list, jotting down notes, sometimes paragraphs, giving her the answers she was missing, moving on to the next before he had a chance to think about the one before in an effort to outrun the horror.

When he'd finished he let go a shuddering breath.

Then he padded into her room and kissed her on the shoulder, leaving the pages on the pillow beside her.

She *still* didn't budge. Sleeping the sleep of the content. Of someone whose life was just as it should be.

He ran a hand over her shoulder, feeling the innate warmth that flowed just below the surface, like the crushed petal of a rose. In touching her, a soft milky scent rose up to him. The tattoo on her shoulder brushed rough against the pad of his thumb. He traced it distractedly. And then not so distractedly.

She deserved better. More. He wanted her to know it. Needed to know she was as amazing as he knew she was. And there was only one way he could think of to tell her. To show her. To make her see.

Spurred, he pressed himself to standing, pieced together his clothes, threw them on only as decency demanded, and headed out through her door, closing it softly behind him.

* * *

The following Tuesday evening Saskia brought a hot chocolate into the lounge and sat, curling her toes beneath the skirt of her maxi dress.

Ernest padded in from wherever he'd been foraging and turned three times before settling on his doggy bed. The fire crackled softly, now she'd got the hang of it, and her new second-hand lounge chairs were gorgeous: red-and-white checked, with pale green and baby blue and soft yellow floral cushions—a riot of spring colour. *Busy,* her dad would have called it, and frowned, thinking of her mother, claiming it gave him a headache. Saskia would have exchanged it for something less lovely. Less *her.*

She'd added touches of riot everywhere the past few weeks, fancying up the relatively blank canvas until it looked to her like the very image of happiness.

Thanks—very much—to Nate. He'd not only given her the opportunity to get out from under the weight of her debt, he'd pulled her from the even more debilitating hit she'd taken to her self-esteem after Stu. And those who'd come before.

She picked up the slightly rumpled pages of yellow legal paper covered in her swirly writing and Nate's sexy scrawl—rumpled because she'd rolled over on them when reaching out for him to find not him but this gift.

She couldn't for the life of her fathom what had changed his mind about answering her interview questions, but he had. He'd written about his interactions with women—the respect, the intrigue, the unashamed temptation. But she could feel his desire to be better. Do better. To become the man he hoped to be. And giving her this he'd given her himself.

No wonder he was always rubbing his temples in frustration, she thought, with all he had in his head. No wonder he worked himself to distraction. No wonder he'd come looking for her.

And Saskia couldn't have loved him more for it.

It had been coming, brimming, easing, falling, pressing in

on her from every angle. Her love for this man who had no clue that he gave so much and took so little for himself. This man who knew his strengths but couldn't see his worth.

How could she know him and not love him? And she'd be so good for him. Take care of him. Relax him. Show him contentment. Make him happy. Love him all his days and nights. If only he'd let her.

Never having been there before, she had no idea what came next. So she sat in the middle of it, feeling it, living it, revelling in it, till her backside turned numb from sitting in the same spot too long.

Ernest leapt from his doggy bed and took off. A moment later a knock sounded.

By the time she reached the door Saskia's heart was thumping through her chest at the thought that it might be Nate. What would she say about what he'd given her? Would he even know what it meant to her? Could it be why he'd done it?

"Earn your keep, Fido, and learn how to open the door!" Lissy called from the other side. Then added, "Men suck!" as she spilled through the door, arms laden with grocery bags—hence the non-use of her key. She gave Ernest a perfunctory cuddle with one foot as she trudged in.

Not all of them, Saskia thought, the bliss riding high again.

"More than usual?" Saskia asked, padding into the kitchen to make another hot chocolate.

"Bamford dumped me."

Wow. Lissy, of the glorious mane of blonde hair with its now hot pink tips, the big blue eyes and curves for the ages, was a bombshell. Crazy, for sure, but men didn't seem to care. As if they couldn't use their brains while their tongues lolled out of their mouths.

"Did he say why?"

Lissy waved a dismissive hand over her shoulder. "Something about compatibility. A lack of seriousness. Blah-blah-blah."

As Lissy upended her bag of groceries on the kitchen table Ernest thought he'd died and gone to heaven—caramel popcorn, butterscotch ice cream, boxes of Oreos.

"You disagree?" Saskia said, plopping a mound or two of chocolate powder into a mug.

Lissy deflated into a chair. "I'm not sure, to tell the truth. Bam was fun. A crazy kind of challenge. But when I see you and Nate together—the chemistry, the way you complement and challenge and fit—there's this aura, like the glow of possibility, that gleams around you. I want that."

Stunned into silence because it really wasn't all in her head, Saskia flinched when the door was knocked upon again. She glanced in its direction, wanting to press Lissy for more about the glowing and the aura.

The knock sounded at the door again.

"If that's Bam, I'm not here," said Lissy as she plonked herself at the kitchen table.

"Why would he think you were?"

Her eyes narrowed a moment. "I told him this was where I'd be if he realised he'd just made the biggest mistake of his life and decided to send flowers or diamonds."

Saskia shook her head at the logic, or lack thereof, then in a kind of daze went to answer the door.

She didn't even notice Ernest was nowhere to be seen until she swung the door open and found herself face-to-face with—

"Stu?"

"Hey, Sas. How's it hangin'?"

Chagrin had brought dimples to his cheeks. Add that to the elegant height, the puppy-dog eyes, the Byronesque mien, the guy was better-looking than a man had a right to be. But looking at him now—at the way his eyes darted anywhere but at her, at the defensive slump of his shoulders, the shuffling of his feet—Saskia wondered how she'd ever dated him at all.

"Aren't you gonna invite me in?"

Her heart beat in her ears and her vision narrowed to about

a square metre in front of her eyes as, watching Stu she felt like Alice watching her old life from the other side of the looking glass.

"Why on earth would I do that?"

He blinked.

"What are you doing here, Stu?"

When he didn't look as if he had plans to go anywhere else, she let him in. Then followed in a kind of haze as he walked into her apartment, making appreciative noises about the work she'd done. He poked his head into her lounge room, glanced at her new TV—not as big as the last, but new all the same—then at Ernest, who was curled up in his cosy bed, pouting. It seemed she wasn't the only one hanging onto reality by a fingernail.

"Hey, boy," Stu said, taking a step Ernest's way.

But Saskia put herself bodily between the man and *her* dog. "Hands off."

He backed up in shock. "Steady on."

"Steady…?" She barked out a laugh, encroaching while he continued to back away. "Stu, you stole from me. And more than just my things. You're so lucky I felt like so much of a fool after you left that I didn't press charges."

His soft brown eyes slanted back to hers before flickering quickly away.

"You know it too. So why on earth have you come back?"

He looked at her, hard, and she saw the cool beneath those warm eyes. The calculation. God, the guy must have seen her coming from a mile away.

"And if you even dare say you missed me—"

"I wasn't going to."

She flinched, but she didn't let him see it. "Spit it out, Stu, and then you can get the hell out of my house."

He took a breath, his lean chest lifting and falling, his expression more hangdog than puppy dog. "I'd like to repay my debt."

That time there was no hiding her shock. As long as she'd

known him he hadn't made a cent from anything other than unemployment benefits. "Wow. Did you sell something? Apart from my gear, I mean? Did you sell your book?"

The flicker of surprise in his eyes told her he'd probably not written another word of the mysterious text.

"Then how? Five dollars a fortnight out of your dole payment? It would take you years."

He lifted his chin as if she'd wounded his pride. "If that's what it takes."

The idea of having this man in her life for all that time, of getting fortnightly reminders of the fool she'd been, made her want to rip her new TV off the wall and give it to him if it meant never to having to see him again. And by the look of him he'd have taken it too.

"You should know I am so pissed off right now—even more than when you left if that's at all possible. So before I tie you to the chair and call the cops, tell me: why are you here? Honestly."

"It was made clear to me that this was my only option."

"*Clear?* By *who?*"

A flash of malice crossed his face before he reached into the back pocket of his torn jeans and pulled out a business card. A card with "BonAventure Capital" written in a perfect black font on a perfect white card.

"I don't understand."

"That guy Mackenzie came and saw me yesterday. We had a conversation about responsibility and recompense."

If the card hadn't convinced her Nate was involved in Stu's reappearance, that did.

"He told me to come here, to pay you back, to…*apologise*, or else."

"Nate *threatened* you?"

"Not in so many words. He made it clear he was a better judge of my priorities than I was."

The irony was not lost on her. She'd spent the better part of a year believing—erroneously—that she'd convinced Stu she was the better judge of what was good for him, while Nate had actually convinced him with one conversation.

She didn't realise she was rubbing at her temple until she'd pressed her thumb to the spot hard enough to leave a mark. Why? Why would Nate have done this to her?

Did he want *his* money back? It made no sense.

Her phone rang. She instinctively rose then she heard Lissy take it. She'd forgotten Lissy was even there. It brought her back to reality with a thud.

"I'd like you to leave, Stu. And this time please don't ever come back."

"But—"

"I'll deal with this," Saskia said, flicking at the corner of the business card.

"So that's it? You're not calling the cops?"

"You really think I would have strapped you to a chair?"

He glanced at the plump love seat behind her, and of everything he'd told her that day it was the only thing that made her smile. Despite all his nasty words, he actually thought her strong enough to take care of *herself.* From that moment on she was certain she'd never forget it either.

"Go," she said, pointing at the door, "before I change my mind."

He nodded. Smarter than she'd ever given him credit for. Then, as he made to move, he said, "You're different. It suits you."

"While you're exactly the same."

He took it as the insult it was meant to be, then walked out through her door. And this time she couldn't have been happier to see him go.

On wobbly legs Saskia moved to the lounge and sat. Ernest uncurled himself from the bed and came over to rest his chin on her knees. She rubbed his soft wiry ears. "I know, boy. I know. But this is better. Beyond better."

A minute later Saskia felt Lissy sink down on the chair beside her.

"You okay?"

Saskia lifted her head to look into her friend's big worried eyes. "I'm fine. We're both fine—aren't we, Ernie? We're survivors. We'll be just fine."

"Men suck," said Lissy.

"Some," Saskia said, as she rubbed noses with Ernest before he padded off to the kitchen in search of crumbs. "Some stick up for you when you least expect it. Who was on the phone?"

"Nate."

Nate.

"I said you'd call him back."

Saskia let out a long, slow breath. One man situation sorted; a whole other one to endure. She'd thought her relationship with Stu was complicated, but now it seemed two-dimensional and black-and-white compared with the situation with Nate.

When Saskia made to stand Lissy pressed her back to the couch. "Leave it for a bit. Catch your breath. Have a glass of wine. Hell, have a bottle. Nate can wait."

"You know what?" Saskia said, standing. "I'm done waiting."

She felt as if she'd been waiting her whole life for men to make up their damn minds. A little pressure here, a nudge or two there, giving them the time, the place, the opportunity, the incentive, the dossier with its encouraging white spaces, the yellow legal pad covered in blatant questions so that they'd open up to her, let her in, love her. And none of it had worked.

She tossed a jacket over her maxi-dress, pulled on the closest pair of shoes at hand, stuck a scarf round her neck and a hat on her head and grabbed her bag.

It was time she did this face-to-face, woman to man, to stop tiptoeing and just have it out.

Saskia worked her way through the maze of Nate's home, up three stairs, turn right, down seven, split levels and closed doors, thinking how hard the guy made it to get into his home, much less his life.

Finally she was out in the wide open living area, all blonde wood trim and gunmetal-grey paint. The ceiling was all vicious angles and the place smelled of chopped wood and leather and a spice she couldn't name. No warm-blooded human being would ever choose to live there. And yet Nate did.

She saw him in the kitchen, tasting something he was cooking on the stove. It stopped her short. He cooked? How had she not known he cooked? And it smelled…amazing. It smelled like the best of Mamma Rita's.

But she was not to be deterred by the fact the man could cook…

When Saskia threw her bag—containing the legal pad and dossiers for incontrovertible proof should she need it—on the slab of rock that constituted his kitchen bench, Nate looked up.

"Men suck!"

He stood taller, wiping a towel across his mouth. "Why, thank you."

"Bamford dumped Lissy, you know."

"I didn't, in fact."

"Yet you don't seem shocked. Why? Lissy rocks. He was lucky to know her, much less…the rest!"

"She does. He was. But you have to admit they were an unlikely couple."

Unlikely? No more unlikely than a hippy statistics maven and the King of Collins Street. At that she began to pace.

"Would you like a drink?" he asked, tilting his chin at a bottle of red wine. "Can I take your hat? Scarf? Jacket?"

She glanced down at her outfit and blinked. From the floppy felt hat to the floaty beige dress, the dressy caramel jacket, ancient multi-coloured scarf and the knee-high ugg boots she only ever wore at home, she looked like the result of a market stall explosion. Whipping off the layers and tossing them at a bar stool, she wondered what she'd been thinking. *Oh, that's right...*

"On the subject of men sucking..."

She pulled the card from her bag and tossed it to him. Damn jock snapped it out of the air easy as you please.

"Why?" she asked, and that one word was filled with more emotion than she'd thought any one word could be. Because his response would give her the answer she'd wanted more than any other in her entire life.

"Closure."

And like a whip across the face she got it. *Closure.* Of course. Right in the moment she realised she was in love with the guy he was plotting his extrication. The end. *Finito.*

It was Stu all over again. Only this time he wasn't making off with her TV while she was out working. He was taking her heart, in broad daylight, right in front of her face.

Knees buckling, she sat on a wooden barstool. Hard.

Nate moved around the bench and slowly slid to the stool beside hers, his knees close enough that she could feel his latent heat.

"Why?" she said, needing more, needing every last skerrick of data to understand fully.

"You're better than him. Better than any man who needs a restraining order to keep him away from you. Better than every damn bozo you pass on the street. I thought you needed to look Stu in the eye to see that. To know you're better off without a TV, without a fridge, without a coffee maker if it means not being with a man like him."

Her eyes flickered to his to find his blue eyes serious. No

charm, no pretence, just Nate. And even while everything inside her felt as if it was unravelling her love for him was like a constant warm hum.

"Then you didn't find him to get your money back."

His raised eyebrows reminded her he'd met the guy.

"Or in the hopes I'd want to get back together with him?"

This time Nate looked as if *he'd* been slapped. Better at her at the dissembling thing, he pulled himself together far quicker, his jaw hardly clenching as he said, "Why? Are you?"

"Good God, no!"

He breathed out long and slow, and his voice was a little raw when he said, "You don't let me get away with anything, and yet you let him get away with what he did. So I wondered if maybe it was because he…he meant more."

"No," she said. The warm hum was getting louder, fuelled by a new and faint hope that maybe, just maybe, Nate actually cared. "He didn't. He doesn't."

"Okay, then."

Only fair he had all the data too, Saskia looked at the hands twisting in her lap. "Stu wrote me a note, you know."

"Today?"

"Back then. That was why I didn't chase him down and kick his ass. I didn't want to have to face that…hatred ever again."

"What did it say?" Nate asked, his voice now less raw, as if had Stu walked through the door he'd not have got another foot without having his manhood kicked up into his neck.

It helped. It really did. Especially as she made herself remember the words she'd tried so hard to forget. "He called me emasculating. Controlling. He said that I only ever pretended to care."

"Hell, Saskia—"

"He was right. In his way. I never loved him, and yet I let him move into my home. I do that. I try too hard to be what

I think people need me to be. Because what I am has never been enough."

"Saskia," Nate said again, his eyes fierce as they roved over every inch of her face, "Stu's an ass. A petty, sad, small-minded toad. He tried his damnedest to take something away from you—something he knew he'd never have—your fierce spirit. But he failed. Fool only made you shine stronger still."

She wanted to believe him. She wanted it more than she'd wanted anything in her whole life. To believe not just the words but the sentiment, the tenacity, the *possibility*... But if the men in her life had taught her anything it was that potential was a pipedream.

Take a man as he is, or don't take him at all.

"You think I shine?"

"I know you shine."

"You couldn't have just said so?"

No, his expression said, *he couldn't.* Almost as if he knew she'd read too much into it.

But, hand to his heart, Nate said, "I'm sorry to the tips of my very everything that I forced you to have to see him again."

Her mouth twisted and she couldn't drag her eyes from the hand across his chest. "Do you plan on tracking down all the men who've wounded me?"

"If that's what it takes."

She laughed despite herself. "I keep telling you I don't need you to take care of me."

"And yet once in a while it would be nice if you just shut up and let me." His brows knitted together. Then, "Odd."

Not odd, she thought. Sweet. Darling. But the fact that he couldn't see it, didn't understand what it might mean, scared her silly.

"It's not your job to make up for their shortfalls," she said.

"Not yours either."

"Yeah. I guess you're right."

"I am right. Always."

She coughed out a laugh, her eyes landing on her bag with the legal pad therein—all the things he'd revealed whether he'd wanted to or not.

"Not always."

"Oh, really?"

"Every mistake I've made has been in a full-bodied effort to find my place, my people. While you have it all, right at your fingertips, and you're determined to throw it away."

She felt Nate still even before her eyes swung back to his. *You have me too,* she said with her eyes. *If you want me.* But the stillness didn't abate. If anything it cooled about ten degrees, and she knew she had her answer. Even if he saw, even if he had any kind of sense of how she felt, he clearly didn't want to.

"I appreciate it," he said. "I do. From afar."

She'd never seen him look more like granite personified. He looked as if he'd been born of the grey walls and blond wood, and faux taxidermy. Maybe that was what the designer had seen. The *true* heart of the man—cold as any stone.

"I wonder if you know how far away you are. You're way over there. And you don't let anybody come close. Not your gorgeous family, who adore you to their very ends. And certainly not me. Paying me off, bringing me Stu, reminding me every two seconds that the end is nigh. Love isn't poison, Nate. It won't kill you. It's natural, it's complicated, its crazy-making, but it's a fact of life."

"Like death and taxes."

Saskia threw her hands in the air and swore like a sailor. "Why the hell am I bothering? You're a lost cause. I knew it, and still it didn't stop me."

"Stop you, what?"

"Oh, no. All you're getting from me any more is exactly

what I want to give—which right now is less than diddly-squat."

She wouldn't have thought a man could be as still as Nate was in those next moments. While she had so much energy pouring through her she wanted to stamp her feet and throw her arms in the air, he didn't even blink.

Then he said, "You constantly—and I mean constantly—amaze me."

Her eyes cut to his.

"Such a little thing, with so much fight in you."

"It's not fight. It's passion. Verve. *Joie de vivre.*"

One eyebrow slid north. If she'd had a bow and arrow and any kind of athletic skill she'd have shot him between the damn things.

"Nate," she said, her hands out in supplication. *Give me a sign. Give me a break!*

He caught her hands to him and didn't let go. "Cards on the table."

Her heart stopped. From one beat to the next—nothing. Then she curled her fingers into his and her blood began to race. "Fine. You first."

He laughed, the sound soft, raw, the loveliest sound in the entire world. "You started it, sweetheart. Tell me what you came here to say. It'll be okay. I promise."

Saskia breathed out hard. The man had more charm in his little finger than the rest of the population of Melbourne combined. Maybe she could tell him that.

He looked into her eyes. She'd never felt him more present, never seen the real him so clearly in the beautiful fathomless blue.

"I'm just a man, Saskia. Flesh and blood and instinct. I don't know what you want unless you tell me."

She could tell him. She could. It was simple after all.

Name: Saskia Bloom
Age: twenty-eight
Looking for: a way to tell the man sitting before her that she's in love for the first time in her life

She took a breath. Tried to still the centrifuge in her mind. To forget herself. And it was like one of those dreams where she felt a scream rising inside her but no matter how wide she opened her mouth no sound came out.

Nate's eyes flickered between hers, then they softened. He turned her hand over in his and lifted it to his mouth, kissing one palm and then the other before letting her go. "Just as I thought. You're no more ready for this than I am."

No! she screamed inside her head. *I'm ready! I've been ready. For ever and always!*

It was just after Stu's awful visit, and Lissy being dumped, and the surfeit want, the need, the desire—it was all a big mess inside her head. A big mess with a solid centre. When it came down to it the thought of laying her heart on the line and being rejected was more than she could bear.

A tear plopped down her cheek before she'd even felt it well in her eye. She wiped it away with the back of her hand, but another followed.

"Don't cry," Nate said.

It was the closest to begging she'd ever heard from the man.

"I can't do tears."

Which only made her cry more.

With an oath, he pulled her into his arms. She struggled against him, knowing if she softened she was gone. And she was all she had.

"Hush," he said, his breath against her hair.

A second later, maybe ten, the effort of keeping herself strong crumbled.

He kissed her on the forehead and then, as if it simply wasn't enough, lifted her face with a finger beneath her chin and pressed his lips to hers. The silken heat of his touch flowed through her, even while her whole body was rent with tension.

His kiss was lush, lovely, lost in time. Her mind was a whirl of sensation and sadness.

With a groan she slid off the stool, threaded her hands through his hair and sank against him, imprinting herself on him, and him on her, as if it might be the last chance she'd have to commit him to memory, pouring every ounce of love she felt into that kiss in the hope he'd feel it, know it and understand it without having to be hit over the head with it.

When he pulled away the tears kept on coming.

Love me, she thought, *love me, love me, like I love you.*

Smiling—*smiling!*—he pressed her hair from her cheeks. "You'll be just fine, Saskia Bloom. I know it. I knew the first moment I saw your picture. You're content. You have your house, your dog, your work, your friends. Your life is in a groove that's made for you. I envy you that."

"I want…more," she said, as close to admitting anything as she'd come.

He shook his head once, then, looking her right in the eye, said, "When you told me what you wanted in a relationship, back at The Cave that night when you refused to come home with me…?"

Saskia nodded, astounded that it felt like such a long time ago.

"You talked about meeting a guy, moving in together, getting married?"

She nodded again, knowing as she pictured all those things that even then she'd imagined those things with him.

"You never once mentioned being in love."

Saskia stopped nodding. The glorious self-pity fled and she shook her head a little as she tried to unearth that memory in its entirety. "Of course I did."

"No," Nate said. "You didn't."

But she *did*. She wanted to be in love and loved with so much of herself her lungs tightened to fists at the very thought. And yet she couldn't open her mouth and say so.

But *he* was the one with the walls, not her. She wanted him, she loved him—couldn't he damn well stop talking rubbish and look at her? It was pouring out of her!

But with a kiss to the end of her nose he extricated himself from her embrace and stepped back, then another step and then he moved around to the other side of the bench to check his pasta sauce and it felt as if he'd walked a mile.

And his words finally came through. *You'll be just fine,* he'd said. Meaning she'd be just fine without him.

She stood on shaky legs and collected her things. She waited until her throat wasn't so tight she could barely swallow, then said, "Nate?"

He turned, faced her across the kitchen. And she wondered if he knew what she was going to say before she did.

"I don't see how… I'm so sorry, but I can't go to Mae's wedding with you."

"Yeah," he said, frowning at his shoes before looking back at her, all dark and impenetrable, his thoughts kept from her behind the deep, dark tunnel of his eyes. "I wondered about that too."

She just looked at him in silence. Her throat a dry wasteland where words could apparently no longer pass.

"Consider this my breaking off our agreement."

He lifted his hands and tore the air and her heart snapped right in two. She heard it. *Ping* and *crack*. And then a *swoosh* as air filled the crevasse.

"Thank you," she said.

He'd broken her heart and she'd *thanked* him. She might not have pressed charges on Stu, but she'd never thanked the guy! She was clearly way more screwed up than she'd thought.

Nate said, "It's been my absolute pleasure."

And with that she turned and walked away.

As she drove off in her newly fixed old car she was glad it seemed to know the way home because her mind was anywhere but on the road.

Reliving every second, every nuance, every touch, every glance, she felt as if Nate had known why she'd come, and he'd carefully turned her about until she no longer knew what she was thinking.

Before she'd gone over there it had felt so much like love. Now it hurt like love, it burned like love, but with her genetic make-up—a transient femme fatale and a shut-in who pined his life away—who the hell was *she* to know?

CHAPTER TEN

NATE SAT ON the couch in his office in battered old track pants and a tank, trainer-clad feet on the coffee table, head resting on the back of the couch. His yoga mat remained curled up in the cupboard, along with his free weights and a folded-up rowing machine, while the sun set over Melbourne, sending long shadows across the room and turning his blue-and-white office a dreamy pinkish-gold.

Nate nudged his shoes off by the heels and slowly lowered his feet to the carpet. It was even softer than it looked. No wonder it had cost a mint. Hitching his pants, he curled his toes into the pile and closed his eyes.

And not for the first time in the past few days, behind his closed lids he saw Saskia.

This time it was barefoot, not five metres from where he sat, the sun shining through her unassuming clothes, revealing a figure you'd never guess would be hidden underneath that op-shop exterior.

Then he saw her lying back in his bed, dark tousled hair splayed out on his pillow, eyes sleepy ten and sensual as she looked up at him, hooked a hand behind his neck and pulled him down to make love to her.

He saw Saskia, her eyes fierce as she told him to loosen up, to open up, accept ruffling, to be a human being.

He saw Saskia, her face mottled with tears as she told him it was over.

ALLY BLAKE

"Here you are."

Nate looked up to see Gabe, laptop bag over his shoulder as he prepped to head home for the day.

"Where else would I be?" It was meant to be a joke, but in the beat of silence both were all too aware it was the blatant truth of Nate's life.

"Beer?" Nate asked.

"Don't have to ask me twice." Gabe dropped his bag and liberated two bottles from the bar below Nate's bookshelves. He snapped the tops off the bottles, sank down on the other end of the couch and said, "So, out with it."

Nate finished a mighty swig, then said, "With what?"

"The reason you're sitting here pouting like a little girl."

No point denying it. "Saskia and I broke up." Knowing it was one thing. Saying it out loud made it feel real. Right behind his ribs. He took another swig.

"She with whom you were never actually going out?"

"Seems we were in the end."

"Yeah, I know."

"How's that?"

"Gut told me. And Paige confirmed it. According to her, you're seriously cute when you're in *lurve.*"

"I'm not in…*anything.* As evidenced by the fact that I am no longer seeing her."

"Lady's choice?"

Nate thought back to their conversation a few nights before. Okay, so he'd thought it over a lot. Over and over. The twists and turns, the moments when he'd felt as if it was about to fall the other way before it flipped again, leaving his chest tight. He'd thought clinching an impossible investment deal was a rush, but being with Saskia was that times a thousand.

Had been, he reminded himself. Then took another swig.

"Yeah." Gabe answered himself, giving Nate a thump on the shoulder. "Man, I'm sorry. I liked her. Paige liked her. Mae was on the verge of asking her to be another bridesmaid. Now, *that* woman is off her tree. If she wasn't Paige's best friend..."

"Poor Clint," they said in unison.

Laughter followed and Nate knocked his bottle against Gabe's. Friendship healed. And it felt good. A relief, even. A need met.

Even while he told himself he needed nothing but the business he'd built, the independence he'd earned, life was better with Gabe in it.

In fact life had been better these past weeks than he remembered it being in a long time. Simpler. Lighter. Easier. He'd seen more of his family than he had in months. His circle of friends—not merely acquaintances but actual friends—had grown without him even realising it, and it felt good.

And he'd had Saskia to thank for it all.

"Wedding's Saturday, remember? So who's the lucky girl you'll be taking now?"

Nate sat forward, rubbed his hands over his face. "No one I guess. I'll go alone."

"Don't say it too loud. The Mackenzie women *will* hear."

"Tough luck. I'm done."

"No more breaking hearts and taking names? Love her, don't you?"

Beyond feigning ignorance as to whom Gabe was referring, Nate moved his gaze to a spot in the middle distance. "I like her. I like being with her. I think about her when I'm not with her. She's bossy, and I like that. But..." The fight seeped out of him as the truth seeped in. "Not that I have anything to compare it to."

"Comparison's not the point, mate. You don't love her or you do."

The sun must have dropped below the horizon because the sensor lights in his office flickered on, casting a cool glow over the room. "Not that it makes any difference. As much as we drive each other crazy…we'd drive each other crazy."

"And that's a bad thing?"

It was messy, challenging, a fight he couldn't always win. It was full-on, distracting, time-consuming. It was emotional, painful, exhilarating. It was anything but bad. It was the most fun he'd had his entire adult life.

"Welcome to the club, mate; your pass and monogrammed towel are in the mail," said Gabe.

"Too bad I spent my last hour with her carefully convincing her there was nothing between us then."

"Ain't over till the fat lady sings."

"So why do I get the feeling I've turned up at the opera house a day late and a dollar short?"

Gabe gave Nate a pat on the back and curled him into a bear hug that thumped the breath from his lungs. Then, clearing his throat, pressed to his feet with a speed that belied his size. "You're coming Saturday." It wasn't a question.

"I think the best gift I could give Mae and Clint would be my *not* coming."

With a final slap on the cheek, like an old Italian mamma, Gabe left Nate to his misery. To the knowledge that he loved a woman who didn't love him. Or, by the dawning realisation in her eyes, didn't love him enough.

He sank his head into his hands and rubbed at his temples. Damn her big brown eyes. She'd turned him soft and then sent him off into the world a great big marshmallow.

Only it didn't make him feel soft. He felt strong with it. As if he'd been running on quicksand his whole life and now the ground beneath his feet had solidified, letting him slow down, see the world as it happened not as a blur as he chased the future.

Saskia. Sweet, interfering, dogmatic, stubborn, gorgeous Saskia. Who'd lived her life on quicksand too. He wondered

if she knew it. If she felt it. If that was what she'd seen in him.
A like soul. Her match. His complement.

Yet still she'd walked away.

And he'd let her go.

It was the night before the wedding and, as Nate tended to do,
he leant in the doorway while the women in his life took over
his mum's lounge room—Jasmine with her eyes flicking to
her twin boys, playing with his old train set, making sure they
weren't hatching plots for world domination, Hope reading an
eBook with her legs hanging over the leg of the couch, Faith
flicking channels on the TV so fast it made Nate's head spin.

When his temple began to throb he did something about
it, grabbing the remote out of Faith's hand and switching off
the damn TV.

Faith's "Hey!" got everyone's attention.

Good. He had something to say.

They wouldn't like it. In fact they might all turn on him.
But he couldn't not say it. He'd *not* said quite enough things
the past few days, and it was eating him from the inside out.

"I have a confession." With that four sets of sharp feminine
Mackenzie eyes swung his way.

Jasmine spoke first and, grinning, said, "Do tell, oh, brother
mine."

"It's about Saskia."

"I *knew* it!" Faith said, her squeal near breaking the sound
barrier.

Hope, meanwhile, gave him a small smile, a tilt of her head,
encouraging him to go on.

"Saskia and I were never actually dating." No, not exactly
true. And this was a time for truth. The idea of anything else
made him feel more exhausted than a man with his youth,
stamina and ripping good health had a right to feel. "Not in
the way we made you believe we were."

"I don't understand," his mother said as she came to sit on

the arm of the chair nearest him, her forehead creased with concern, her heart in her eyes.

The threat of emotion swarmed over him, but rather than pressing it back, pretending it didn't exist, he merely held it at bay, letting it lift and subside like a lunar tide.

"I found her online with the express purpose of taking her to Mae's wedding as my date, merely to keep you lot from finding one for me."

Silence stretched to the outer reaches of the big room, broken only by the click and whir of the old wooden train set, whose batteries were winding down.

"I don't understand," said his mother.

"It was fake," Faith said, as if trying to make sense of it herself. "The relationship. The affection. The attraction. All of it."

Not all of it, no. But he knew them well enough to know any flicker of hope would be fanned into a flame. So he chose his words carefully.

"We made a deal that was mutually beneficial to us both."

"Good God, you *paid* her?" Faith asked, incredulous.

"Don't say it like that," he bit out, turning on Faith so fiercely her eyes bugged out of her head. He reined himself in a notch. "Don't even think it. The details of our agreement are none of anybody's business but our own. But, since we involved you in the ruse, it's fair that you know the only reason she went along with it as long as she did was because she had this crazy compulsion that I needed her help."

"If anyone needs help it's you, brother." That was Hope.

Nate puffed a laugh from his nose, grateful she was in the room. Grateful they all were, to tell the truth, and that he could finally say what he had to say. And by the way they were listening they would know he meant it.

"I wasn't thinking anything bad about her, Nate," Faith said, drawing his eye. "I've met her, remember? She's way too cool for you. But I *am* flabbergasted that my darling, dashing big brother actually thinks any woman would need an inducement to be with him."

God, was that a tear? He couldn't take tears.

"Faith, you've missed the point. I went miles out of my bloody way to find a woman to *not* be with me."

That met with silence.

"I don't want marriage. I don't want a partner." His hand was running up the back of his hair before he could stop himself. "I want to date who I want and when I want; without you all—or anyone, in fact—expecting it might one day lead to me settling down. It's just *never* going to happen."

"Why?" his mother asked, rising now to take his hand, to look into his eyes. "The truth. All of it."

Jasmine had one of her boys, was hugging him tight, as if telling herself her own son would never feel that way. Faith watched, tears at the corners of her eyes. Hope breathed evenly, smiled softly and simply waited, as if she'd been waiting for the truth—all of it—all her life.

"I was there," Nate said. "After Dad died. Missing him, mourning him. I still think about him every day." He fisted a hand in the front of his sweater. "But I don't *ever* want to feel that much need and hurt and empathy and rage and love and fear again."

Hope slid gracefully to her feet and came over and gave him a hug. Then punched him hard enough on the arm to hurt. "We know. We watched in dazed amazement how our little big brother handled himself. You were the glue and we may have overused you. For that I apologise. Profusely."

She looked to the others, who all nodded with her.

"But, for the record, while you're stuck with us—interfering, emotional and fabulous as we are—finding that one person out there in the big wide world who you *choose* to be with…well, that's something else entirely. Love is scary and magical and bittersweet and special and hard and wonderful and the best thing that can ever happen to you in life."

He looked around at his sisters—all strong women. All nodding. All of whom had come out the other side, able to throw their hearts into the ring. All hopeful he might still.

And even while he ought to have been setting up a whiteboard, with graphs and charts and a loud hailer to explain how and why it was different for him...all he could think of was Saskia.

Saskia, whom he'd chosen to be in his life, even if only for a finite time. Saskia, who pushed him and challenged him and laughed with him, made room for him. Saskia, who made him feel light and funny and free. Saskia who made him *feel*.

Bittersweet didn't even begin to describe the pleasure and the pain. The pleasure of knowing her. The pain of losing her.

Hell.

"I have to go," he said, his voice raw.

"Yeah, yeah, yeah," said Faith as she gathered up the remote.

Hope shot him a wink before sliding down onto the floor to play train smash with the boys. And Jasmine, relieved of duty, leant back against her wall and closed her eyes.

"We heard you, darling. No more matchmaking," his mother promised as she walked him to the door. "Though you can never make us promise not to hope you'll one day find her. Or that maybe you already have."

"Mum—"

"You've said your piece. My turn. You always were such a stubborn boy. Once you put your mind to something—whether it was building the best linen fort ever seen, or looking after all of us after Nathan died—that was it. Your father was stubborn too, you know. But his stubbornness was inclusive. And even though he died too young, he died happy. Nurtured. Inspired. Deeply touched by love. I'd hate to see you regret any choices you might have made in powering that stubborn streak with fear, not love."

She gave him a kiss, then near shoved him out through the

door—likely so his womenfolk could dismantle every word he'd said. Either way, he *had* said his piece.

Crazy that the hardest part had been admitting that he and Saskia had been faking it. Maybe because amidst the hard truths that was a big fat lie.

He waited for dread to set in at the very thought, but instead felt…nothing. As if the tide of emotion that had swelled earlier had abated, leaving him bereft. Empty. Missing her. Her warmth, laughter and charm. The way she kissed, the way she melted against him, her feelings for him gleaming from her honest brown eyes.

He shoved his hands in the pockets of his jeans and took a deep breath of fresh air—and reminded himself of the likelihood he'd never see her again.

Now she was gone. Gone from his life. His days. His nights. His everything.

And like *that* the dread was there. Engulfing him like a wave of fury that he could have been so stupid.

His mother was right. And Hope. And even Faith.

He *did* use his obstinacy as a shield. He *did* need help. And Saskia *was* way too cool for him.

And yet he was in love with Saskia Bloom. He loved the woman with a conviction and certainty he could no longer deny. And he'd seen it in her eyes, felt it in her touch, tasted it in her tears—she'd been right there with him in every possible way.

Afraid to love, afraid not to.

"Hell," he said, this time out loud, and he kicked the porch so hard he limped out to the car.

Saturday morning Saskia headed to Dating By Numbers, her infographic in tow.

She could have emailed—it would have taken five seconds flat—but she wanted to see Marlee. The woman might be part shark, but she was smart, she had knowledge, and she'd seen through Saskia in a red-hot second. If anyone could smack her out of this funk it would be the wizard behind the pink curtain.

"Saskia," Marlee said, with honest pleasure in her eyes before she hid it behind a cool smile.

"I wanted to give you this." Saskia had framed it. It was a work of art—quite simply the cutest thing Lissy had ever whipped up.

Marlee's eyes roved over the hopeful colour, the joyful curlicues, the straight stats and romantic hooks, a smile lighting her eyes as she saw "follow your heart" scrawled across the bottom.

"Thank you. It's darling."

"So glad. Take a day to look it over, in case you want any changes, then I'll send it to the digital marketing team and get it moving."

Marlee looked over at Saskia, her eyes narrowing as she took the whole of her in. It seemed jaunty knee-high boots, skinny jeans, winsome floral top and fabulous faux fur jacket had been pipped by blurry eyes and a permanent crease above the nose.

"Coffee?"

"Sure." Why not? She had nowhere else to be.

Saskia followed Marlee into her office. Bit her lip. Held her breath. Then spat out the question that had been hovering on her lips since the moment she'd decided to come calling. "Can I ask you one last thing?"

"What's that?"

"How many find The One?"

"You want numbers?" Marlee asked, a red talon flicking towards the screen of her computer.

"I want...*hope*."

Marlee turned, coffee forgotten. "Then the numbers don't matter. The odds against only exist because of the odds for. In the end all that matters is you. And your guy. The rest is gravy."

"Gravy."

Taking Saskia by the hands, Marlee led her to a big squishy white couch in the corner. "I wasn't going to say, but last time you were here I would have bet my fortune you'd been struck by cupid's arrow. Now you look like you've been hit by a truck, which then backed up and ran over you again. What happened?"

What happened? Even she wasn't sure. She'd thought over that last conversation so many times, yet couldn't get a grasp on what had gone wrong. What she'd missed. She just felt right deep down in her gut that there had been a moment when she could have had it all, and instead she'd let it slip through her fingers.

She'd been so sure she loved Nate—until he'd convinced her otherwise. And yet days later it still felt like love, it still hurt like love, burned like love and yet she still couldn't be sure.

Saskia took a deep breath, then said, "I met a man—"

"On my site?"

Saskia nodded. "I met a man, dated him, fell in love—and screwed it all up."

"Happens every day."

"Heartening."

"Mmm. You know what else happens every day? People realise the errors of their ways and make up for it."

"How?"

"Any which way they damn well can."

"You're good at this. Are you married? I'm sorry. It's none of my business."

"No, I think that's a fair question, considering what I peddle. I *was* married. Many years ago. To a bear of a man with a big prickly beard and a laugh that stopped time. He passed away too young. And I've never found it again. Maybe because I had my one chance, or maybe because I've never put myself out there."

Saskia looked at the woman. Beneath her class and elegance and her sharp tongue she nursed a broken heart.

"My father lived with a broken heart," Saskia said, "his whole life. I always thought it rather romantic. And thus spent my whole childhood trying to make up for it, getting nothing in return. I thought that was love, but now I wonder if I haven't been completely reactionary—treating every relationship as an 'I'll show you, you mean bastard.' As if even *one* of them loved me it would prove, to a dead man, that I was right and he was wrong."

"Understandable," Marlee said.

"Yeah—'understandable' has pretty much driven me my whole life. But it hasn't helped me sleep much the past few days."

"In my experience nothing beats a warm pair of male arms for that." Marlee patted her on the hand and went to get the coffee.

Marlee was right—each person reacted as they chose to react and each had to live with the consequences.

As she thought about her choices to date and their consequences, and Nate—out there, loved and not knowing it. For her there was no choice.

"I want love," she said out loud. Then louder, arms out to the world, as if she'd been born again, "I'm Saskia Bloom and I want to love *and* be loved."

Marlee hovered in the doorway, her smile soft before it spread into a grin. "Now, this poor fellow we quite purposely have neglected to mention, is he a man of unparalleled excellence? Is he a man of manners and charm and fantastic genes? Is he a possibility partner for life?"

She'd never looked for a partner.

Sharing herself, leaning on him, taking his advice, listening to him—none of that had much come into it. Until Nate. That strong, blind, charming, heartbreaking, stubborn, oak of a man had never let her get away with steering on her own. He'd imposed himself as much on the relationship as she had. In equal measure.

As if the curtains had been parted and the light let in, suddenly a whole new possibility opened up to her—the possibility of a life not for him but *with* him.

It felt like a brave new world. Was she brave enough to see it through? If any man had made her feel safe enough to try it was Nate. Vulnerable enough to love it was Nate. Happy enough to let him take care of her as much as she took care of him it was Nate.

She didn't need Marlee to give her hope. She had more than enough to push her from the chair, give Marlee a hug and a kiss, and walk...no, *run* from the room.

It was just after ten on the first Saturday in spring. She had a date.

CHAPTER ELEVEN

THAT WAS A hundred-dollar blow-dry wasted, Saskia thought as she wobbled down the stone steps that led to Blairgowrie Beach, one hand on her hair, trying to keep the once slick waves from turning wild in the whipping wind.

As for the dress—foxy, floaty, seriously *va-va-voom* and chosen to blow Nate's socks off—it suddenly felt too fantastical, too sexy, too lacking in fabric for a beach wedding on a blustery spring day. Not surprising since she'd bought the thing when high on burgeoning love.

Goosebumps danced up and down her arms. But there was no going back now. She was there on a mission. She was a strong woman, a business-owner, a home-owner, a DIY decorator who had laid her own bathroom tiles. She had a tattoo and had swum with sharks. She could tell a man she loved him even if there was no certainty she'd hear the same back.

Holding herself together—just—she scanned the crowd scattered along the narrow beachfront.

She spotted Paige and Gabe, chatting to an older couple—Mae's parents, judging by the twin sets of vibrant red hair. Lissy and Bamford were there together, but as friends, not lovers, and the two of them were cheerfully laughing at something Lissy had said. Even Clint and Mae were about—Clint chatted with friends in suits, many wearing no shoes, and Mae was on the other side of the crowd, spinning in a slinky backless number, the cool sea air clearly not touching her at all.

And then the crowd parted and there he was. The man she loved.

Seeing Nate after being sure she'd never see him again amazed and terrified her. As for the bone-deep knowledge that she adored the guy and had every intention of making him believe her… That made her knees positively quake.

Especially when he looked the antithesis of ruffled—clean-shaven, with sunlight glinting off his neat dark blond hair, in a suit that made the most of the glory beneath it and with his eyes covered with sexy sunglasses. He looked…perfect.

He brought a glass of champagne to his lips as he turned to survey the crowd, and she knew the moment he spotted her. His hand stilled, his mouth kicked at one corner, and his chest fell as he breathed out long and slow.

The tinkling of laughter, the clinking of champagne glasses, the soft *swoosh* of waves lapping at the shore—faded till all Saskia could hear was the thundering of her heart.

He excused himself, put his champagne on a passing tray, shoved one hand in a trouser pocket and walked towards her. She ditched her heels as they kept sticking in the soft sand and walked towards him, meeting him halfway.

When he came close he took off his sunglasses and she could see the smudges under his eyes, the worry lines etched at their edges. And, since he looked just how she felt, her heart gave a thumpety-thump because it might have something to do with her.

"Hi, Nate," she said, her voice hearteningly strong.

"Saskia."

He leaned in to kiss her cheek and stayed there a beat past familiar. A beat into want. She let her eyes close, filled herself with his warmth and his heady scent. Before she did anything stupid like throw herself into his arms, she pulled away.

"Credibility?" she asked.

His eyes didn't leave hers as a small smile curved the corner of his mouth. "Not this time."

Her heart thudding like a runaway hammer, Saskia glanced over his shoulder at the wedding party in the distance. "I had to come. I couldn't disappoint Mae. She did help me finish my online dating research, after all."

He tilted his chin in understanding and the smile curving at the corner of his mouth kicked a little higher. "Well, I'm glad you came. In fact I have something for you. Brought it just in case."

She looked down to see a small silver bag with frothy silver paper poking out of the top. "You do realise the bride and groom are the only ones meant to be getting gifts today?"

"We got them a toaster."

"Did we, now?" she asked, cool as she pleased, even while her stomach soared at his use of "we." She tried to mentally slap it down but it continued to buzz along happily.

Paige waved to Saskia across the beach, started to move, then saw she was with Nate and took a ninety-degree angle away from her.

Saskia's hand shook as she took Nate's gift. His finger brushed hers and a spark shot between them—the same spark that had been there at the first meeting. The one she'd clung to as she'd fallen deeper and deeper under his disarming charm.

She peeled away the soft silver wrapping to find a solitary bar of goats' milk soap. Her one downfall into decadence. She'd mentioned it maybe once and he'd remembered. And sought it out. And it was near impossible to find. That little shop in the Dandenongs was about the only place you could get it. Meaning he'd gone looking. With her in mind. In an effort to make peace? Or more…?

Blinking, she looked up at him, clueless as to what to say.

"It came in a pack of two," he said. "I kept one for myself. My skin's never felt better."

He smiled his innately charming smile, only this time there wasn't any performance in it. Just him, his eyes roving over her face as if he couldn't quite believe she was there.

When his eyes landed back on hers—blue, hot, hungry—her whole body began to pulse. "Thank you," she said, her voice thick.

"You're most welcome. Now, since I haven't quite got around to finding a standby date, would you care to accompany me?"

He held out his arm; she slid her hand in the crook.

They walked in no particular hurry towards the rest and Saskia said, "I knew you hadn't asked anyone else."

"How's that?"

"Your sister rang just before I came."

"Oh. What did Faith say?" His hand came down on hers, their fingers entwining, and his thumb ran over her wrist, sending waves of heat and hope all through her.

Saskia breathed out, even laughed a tad. "She told me about your family meeting. I'm so proud of you, Nate. Now, hold onto them with everything you have. Know how lucky you are to have them at all."

"I will. I do."

And since he'd given her an opening she saw no reason not to take it. "She also said you were pining."

Nate laughed. "Terror."

"She's softer than you think, you know. She's…" *Hang on a second*. "How did you know it was Faith?"

"I'm sorry?"

"It could have been Hope who'd called. Or Jasmine."

"Hmm?"

Saskia tugged at his arm, pulling them both up short. She held a hand to her eyes to shield them from the sun. Noticing, Nate moved to shield her all on his own.

And then it hit her. "You *asked* Faith to call. To casually let slip you were coming alone."

He looked over her shoulder a moment, before his eyes slanted back to hers. "I figured what's the good of having bumptious sisters who won't butt out of my affairs unless I use them for my own nefarious purposes?"

The sun created a halo around his golden head, leaving his eyes dark smudges in his perfectly carved face. But there was no mistaking the glint, the gleam, the need, want, desire, all shifting below the surface.

"Considering how we left things, I wasn't sure you'd have listened to me."

"I'd have listened, and I'd have come." Saskia grabbed a hold of his lapels and gave the big guy a shake. "And not because of any contract. Just because you asked."

While she still held his jacket so tight, not wanting to let him go ever, Nate lifted a hand. It was millimetres from her cheek, a whisper from her skin, when Mae came barrelling up.

"My God, you two look gorgeous. Don't they look gorgeous?" she said to no one in particular. "I just want to stick you on top of my cake and eat you with a spoon. Later, though. It's all about to begin. If you want to join the crowd over there somewhere I'm about to marry the man of my dreams!"

With that she skipped away, her red hair a riot against the blue sky.

Saskia looked back at Nate to find him watching her, his gaze intent, as if his eyes had never left her. "This isn't a dream," he said. "You're really here."

Happiness tugged at her belly and her heart felt too big for her chest. "I'm really here."

"And you do look gorgeous. Beyond gorgeous. In fact—" He lifted his trouser leg to reveal two pairs of socks. "In preparation for having one pair knocked off."

Saskia laughed, the sound floating away on the sea air. "You were confident I'd come!"

"Hopeful," he said, his hand finally landing on her cheek with such care and affection she leant into his touch, into him.

"To hell with it," he growled, enfolding her hand in his and leading her up the beach and up a grassy sandbank behind a bright blue beach hut with a red roof. He turned her to face him and said, "I drove for an hour to go to a shop to buy stuff to make me smell like the milk of a goat. Washed myself in the stuff for days. Because I missed your scent. I missed you. When what I really should have done is this."

And then he kissed her. Hauling her in tight and drinking her in like a drowning man. Only she was the one drowning. In lush waves of pleasure that swirled behind her eyelids like a kaleidoscope of colour and pulsed through her veins all the way to her toes.

When the kiss softened, slowed, till its sweetness nearly broke her apart, Saskia dropped her head to lean her forehead against the solid wall of his chest, the not so steady beat of his heart mirroring the not so steady beat of her own.

"I'm sorry about the other day," she said. "I was in a messy head space—lots of thoughts clashing. And it's not your fault I fell in love with you. You were very clear about what you wanted. I was the one who stepped outside the rules of the game."

"You what?" His hands went to her cheeks, lifting her face to look into his.

"Stepped outside—"

"The other bit."

She swallowed, thought one last time about feigning amnesia then squared her shoulders and looked him right in the eye. She saw so much possibility and potential in him, in her life with him, and it was too amazing to resist.

"I'm in love with you."

Saskia's mouth fell open. It had been Nate who'd spoken. Nate who now had his hands on her upper arms as if he'd sensed her knees had given way.

"You okay?" he asked.

"Not so much."

Looking around, he found a park bench tucked into a private copse of rough-leaved trees on the edge of the beach, and paid the skateboarders perched thereupon a bunch of notes to rack off.

"You love me?" Saskia said as she sank to the bench, the words thick and unfamiliar on her tongue.

"Yeah," said Nate as he perched on the edge of the seat beside her, "I do."

A glance her way, then he ran a hand up the back of his head. But not in a frustrated way—more in a chagrined way. As if he knew he should have said so a hell of a lot sooner. Then his hand fell to hers, wrapping it tight.

"Saskia, I was living in a tunnel, with no light at the end. Then you came along, and suddenly I noticed when I could smell fresh air, when I felt sunshine. I began to notice the stars and the ground at my feet. You, Saskia Bloom, are my earth."

So much emotion swelled inside her there were no words. Just feelings. So many wonderful, tumbling impossibly beautiful feelings. And the knowledge that she held Nate's heart in the palm of her hand. She knew then that she'd take better care of it than she had of anything else her whole life.

"Before I met you," Saskia said, turning to bump knees, to slide a hand onto his smooth cheek, to look deep into his spellbinding eyes, "I was like a mouse spinning on a wheel— fully expecting to reach my desired destination so long as I kept going in the same direction. And then along came you. You showed me another way." She ran a hand through his hair, smiling when the wind took over, ruffling it just a tad. "I'm not sure what I was ever so afraid of."

"Me either."

"This, perhaps?" she asked, sliding her arms around his waist.

"Not so scary."

"How about this?" she said, sliding her hand over his shoulder as she straddled him. Light played through the trees above, shadows dappling eyes not able to hold back the gleam.

His hands went straight to her backside, held on. "Nope. Not that. How about this for scary: I choose you, Saskia Bloom. If you'll have me."

Scary? Try the very meaning of perfection!

"I'll have you, Nate Mackenzie. And have you and have you and have you."

She dipped her head to kiss him. Shock and awe subsided as he kissed her back tenderly, surely, ravishingly. Her very own big, beautiful, sweet, kind, bold master of the universe.

The hum of music rolled over the sandbank and skimmed the edges of Saskia's love-drenched mind. A grunge version of "Wishing and Hoping."

It was Nate who pulled away and said, "Is that…?"

Her ears pricked up. "The band from The Cave!"

"Mae is a crazy woman."

"I like her."

"Yeah," Nate drawled. "I can't quite believe it, but I do too. Meaning we'd better go do this thing."

Nate lifted her off his lap, placed her gently on the sandy grass and helped her back into her shoes. Then, standing, he put the silver bag in one of Saskia's hands and wrapped his arm about her waist, snuggled her in against his side.

When they hit the beach Saskia marvelled at the crisp, perfect blue of the sky, at the sweet fluffy white of the clouds, at the way the sand sparkled like glitter, and asked the one question she'd wanted an answer to that she hadn't put in her dossier.

"Why did you choose me?" Saskia asked. "From the site, I mean."

"The urge to know what retro grunge meant." He waved a hand at the band rocking barefoot by the waves. "That and the fact you had the sexiest eyes I'd ever seen, the sweetest mouth, the most incongruous hat…"

He leaned down to brush a kiss against her mouth and soon Saskia thought breathing was overrated.

They pulled up at the back of the group, and Nate waited until Mae had skipped down the makeshift aisle before asking, "So why did you choose *me*?"

Saskia almost laughed out loud before she realised he was

serious. Sweet man. "Oh. Well, I near didn't. Don't get me wrong—you were adorable. Got me all tingly with one photo. But you looked so uptight." She looked at him now, pink-cheeked from the wind, hair ruffled, tie askew from her ministrations. *Yeah*, she thought, *he so needed me.* "The only thing that made me think we might have anything in common was that *Catch-22* is your favourite book."

Nate looked at her blankly.

"You said so. In your profile."

"I did?"

"It's not?"

"I work a lot. I don't have much time to read."

"Ha! And to think that tipped the odds in your favour. Imagine if you'd gone for *Valley of the Dolls*. Or *Spot Goes to the Park. Twilight*. Ooh, now *that* would have brought you a whole other type of woman calling."

Nate's warm, strong, insistent arm around her waist tightened, his fingers sinking into the flesh at her waist in warning. As warnings went, it only made her want to ramp things up.

Until he looked deep into her eyes and said, "I don't want another type of woman."

Saskia's breath left her lungs in a whoosh. "Do you always know the exact right thing to say?"

"Famously." He grinned, and his charm beamed across the beach till it outshone the sun. "You'd better get used to it."

He planted a kiss on her mouth, sealing the deal.

As heat blossomed inside her Saskia had a funny feeling she'd never get used to Nate. His kindness and his ambition. His loyalty and resolve. His easy smile and deep convictions. His hot touch and the love that blazed in his eyes.

When Gabe noticed they were behind him he made space and smiled at them in a way Saskia was only just beginning to understand. She looked at Nate to find he was watching her.

Love you, he mouthed.

She snuck in a kiss in response, and it occurred to her she'd found her love formula after all. It was as beautifully simple as all the best formulas: Find someone you love who loves you right back.

Then, as Mae married Clint on that windy sunny beach, Saskia lifted her face to the dappled sun and breathed deep of the sea air, her heart filled with such light, such happiness, she wasn't sure she'd ever get used to either.

Though she was going to have a damn fine time trying.

EPILOGUE

NATE CAUGHT THE toast as it popped out of Saskia's ancient second-hand toaster. He knew what to give her for Christmas. Or maybe he'd just bring his own top-of-the-range one over. He spent most nights at hers, after all. Her espresso machine was a thing of the gods.

But it was more than that. Something about the hot little fireplace and the riot of colour, and the over-soft bed it was simply too difficult to get out of in the morning—especially when it was filled with warm, sleepy Saskia. It was a combination far more him than a fake rhino head on the bathroom wall and stuffy leather.

He lathered the hot bread in chocolate spread, popped a corner and threw it over his shoulder, unsurprised when it didn't hit the floor. The thump of Ernest's tail was as good as asking for more.

"Enough," he said, attempting Saskia's stern but loving tone. Ernest just looked at him as if he was kidding. He threw the dog another corner and took off before the canine had the chance to point those big glistening eyes his way.

Saskia looked up from her computer and smiled. Nate's heart squeezed in his chest. It happened every time he laid eyes on her, and yet he found he couldn't get used to it. Hoped he never would.

He pressed a kiss to her waiting mouth. Her willing heat was no surprise. "I'm off."

"Gabe and Paige are coming for dinner."

"Am I invited?"

She rolled her eyes. "You kidding? You practically live here. I should start charging rent. Or maybe you can just bring your toaster over as a down payment. Mine's on its last legs."

It was a done deal. He perched on the edge of her desk. "Should I consider this the start of negotiations?"

"Sure," she said, her mouth kicking up at one corner. "If that floats your boat."

He pulled her out of her chair and into his arms. "*You* float my boat, Saskia Bloom."

When she'd caught her breath, she said, "Lucky, because you float mine." Her sultry eyes darkened as she leant in for another kiss. Soft, sweet, and soon rocketing into something scorching.

Nate pulled away with a groan. "I have to go. Promised Gabe I'd tag-team. New investment prospect has him in a lather."

Not trusting himself, or her, he pressed her back into her chair. Her feet were tucked instantly up under her, and she snuck a pencil between her teeth. *So damn cute,* he thought. *And sexy and smart and sweet and stubborn.* All must-have traits on his new list for the woman in his life.

She grinned around the pencil and began to swivel her chair back and forth, her knees rubbing against his. Lucky he had a car coming for him in five minutes. He wasn't sure he'd be able to drive in his current state.

As he turned to leave she grabbed him by the sleeve of his shirt, her hand curling around his wrist, sending shards of heat up his arm. To think this hot little gamine creature was his. All his.

He already knew he was never letting her go again.

He'd tell her so later, when she was naked in his arms. Trapped. She tended to be more amenable, less stubborn, after he'd loved her into a pile of molten limbs.

"New gig's just come in," she said, pointing the pencil at her flash new computer monitor.

Completely unable to help himself, he leaned over her, sucking in lungs full of her soft morning scent as he looked at the screen. "What am I looking at?"

"Pegasus Motors have taken us on to do a series of infographics. For starters it seems I'm going to *have* to test-drive their entire range of sports models. You can come along if you like."

"I *knew* there was a reason I loved you."

"Just one."

"Okay, two. Maybe three."

One last kiss, he told himself as her hand snuck around his neck and pulled his mouth to hers.

Three quarters of an hour later he zipped his pants and made a run for the door, cold toast between his teeth, Saskia's old copy of *Catch-22* under his arm for the car ride, and ignoring the constant buzzing of his phone.

He told himself Gabe would have to wait.

Hell, the whole world could wait for all he cared.

A man had to have his priorities straight, after all.

* * * * *

Look out for
Mills & Boon® TEMPTED™ 2-in-1s,
from September

*Fresh, contemporary romances
to tempt all lovers of
great stories*

A sneaky peek at next month...

MODERN™

INTERNATIONAL AFFAIRS, SEDUCTION & PASSION GUARANTEED

My wish list for next month's titles...

In stores from 16th August 2013:

❏ Challenging Dante – Lynne Graham

❏ Lost to the Desert Warrior – Sarah Morgan

❏ Never Say No to a Caffarelli – Melanie Milburne

❏ His Ring Is Not Enough – Maisey Yates

❏ A Reputation to Uphold – Victoria Parker

In stores from 6th September 2013:

❏ Captivated by Her Innocence – Kim Lawrence

❏ His Unexpected Legacy – Chantelle Shaw

❏ A Silken Seduction – Yvonne Lindsay

❏ If You Can't Stand the Heat... – Joss Wood

❏ The Rules of Engagement – Ally Blake

Available at WHSmith, Tesco, Asda, Eason, Amazon and Apple

Visit us Online

You can buy our books online a month before they hit the shops! **www.millsandboon.co.uk**

0813/01

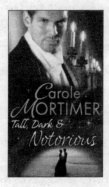

Join the Mills & Boon Book Club

Want to read more **Modern™** books?
We're offering you **2 more** absolutely **FREE!**

We'll also treat you to these fabulous extras:

- **Exclusive offers and much more!**

- **FREE home delivery**

- **FREE books and gifts with our special rewards scheme**

Get your free books now!

visit www.millsandboon.co.uk/bookclub
or call Customer Relations on 020 8288 2888

The World of Mills & Boon®

There's a Mills & Boon® series that's perfect for you. We publish ten series and, with new titles every month, you never have to wait long for your favourite to come along.

Blaze.

Scorching hot, sexy reads
4 new stories every month

By Request

Relive the romance with the best of the best
9 new stories every month

Cherish™

Romance to melt the heart every time
12 new stories every month

Desire™

Passionate and dramatic love stories
8 new stories every month